STIR UP

STIR UP

A Lark Davis Mystery — Book 2

Annabelle Hunter

Stir Up

Lark Davis Mysteries Book 2

Copyright 2019 by Annabelle Hunter

https://annabellehunter.com/

Cover Design by Melody Simmons

Editing by Casey Harris-Parks of Heart Full of Ink

Proof Editing by Josh Stabile

ISBN: 978-1-7330325-1-3 (Book)

ISBN: 978-1-7330325-2-0 (ebook)

Version: 6.14.19

CHECK OUT THESE OTHER WORKS BY ANNABELLE HUNTER

Lark Davis Mystery

Leg Up

Stir Up

Load Up - To be released in September 2019

Barrow Bay Mysteries

Number's Up - To be released in August 2019

DEDICATION

This book is dedicated to my children, my Love and my Joy.

ACKNOWLEDGMENTS

Thank you to all the people who have encouraged me and helped me along this journey:

First to my friends, who supported me with love, support, and a willingness to read. I would be nowhere without them.

Then to all the people that were willing to read and give me their feedback. I have found great friends, writers, and authors through this experience, and I thank you all for every time you were honest with me, even when it meant that you might hurt my feelings.

I'd also like to thank my editor, Casey Harris-Parks, for all her patience, time, and humor. Working with you was a pleasure, no matter how many times you told me to stop using fragments.

And as always, I would like to thank my family for helping and encouraging me, and being so excited that I was taking this step.

CHAPTER 1

Y ou stole my horse!"

The accusation came bellowing down my barn, bouncing off the metal walls as I tucked my newest addition, Bon Voyage VH, into his stall. Patting the bay horse's neck to calm him, I made sure not to react as I unbuckled his halter and let him free to look around. Only once I was sure he would be fine, did I close the stall door and turn to face the newcomer.

"Emily Reed. How nice to see you again." I faked a smile as I greeted the woman storming towards me with a large frown. I hadn't expected this confrontation, but I knew it was a possibility when I took the talented dressage horse and client on. Emily was hot-headed and young, which, in this case, was code for immature and unprofessional. Her storming into my barn to yell at me about a client's decision only proved this. *Way to be a cliché, Emily.*

"YOU STOLE MY HORSE!" Her voice raised another octave, which would've been impressive had she not also poked my chest before stepping into my personal space.

Really? Did she think she would fight me? Please. We were both obsessed with riding to the exclusion of all else. She knew no more about self-defense than I did. Which, as I had learned recently, wasn't much. Turned out punching someone hurt a lot. Life lesson learned.

Emily had the bleached blonde hair that I found common at the top levels of competing in the U.S. where looks tended to matter just as much as talent. We had run into each other a few times on the show circuit, but she believed she was an up-and-coming star and I was just a proven 'no-one,' clinging to the middle ground between international level competition and a good record at high-level shows. At the time, I excused her arrogance. I remembered a time when I, too, was stupid enough to make the same mistake, back before life and divorce had beat it out of me. Now, I was struggling not to match her unprofessional behavior with some of my own.

"One, I didn't steal anything. Your ex-client came to me. I didn't even transport him. Abigail had him brought by a third party, the one you had to have passed coming in. Two, this is my place of work and I try to conduct myself with some decorum within its walls. You might think about doing the same." Lies, all lies. I was rarely professional, and I didn't have more than a passing relationship with decorum, so despite my calm tone, I was seething at the attack. I used my shoulder to push her aside and walked into my tack room, hesitating when I realized I still had Bon's halter and lead rope in my hands. Well, I wasn't going back to the stall with Emily here, so it would have to hang next to the bridles for now. I hung the halter before I turned to face her again, rolling my eyes at her hovering frown.

"He is mine, Lark! I have been training him and taking care of him and... everything! Abby doesn't even know what to do with him. How could she have told you everything? How could she do this without telling me?"

"You are here now. *You* can tell me all those things." I wasn't touching her relationship with Abby.

"No. No! You can't. You can't just *take* him. You can't steal my horse. You can't just... just... take him. I need him back. I need him back now."

"I don't know what to tell you, Emily. Abby made her choice—"

"He is MINE, Lark. I picked him out. I did the training. I raised him! She can't just... She can't! How could you steal him?"

Oh, for goodness sakes! She sounded like she raised him from a colt instead of just flying him over from Europe a few years ago with Abby footing the bill. Already mostly trained. 'Raised him' indeed. I should get a medal for not yelling at her.

"For the last time, I didn't steal anything. Abigail called me two weeks ago and asked if I had a spot in my barn for him. You'll need to take it up with her if you want to know why. I only do what the client wants." Walking over to the dirty bridles from my morning rides, I started cleaning them, refusing to get a horse out while Emily was here. Only Twice, my daughter's mare, was left, anyway. Anything to delay that ride a little longer. On second thought, how long could Emily keep it up? Could I put it off until my lesson got here? No, I was better than that. Maybe.

"Hey, Lark! There's a red truck blocking the…" Missy's voice dropped off when she saw the confrontation between us. Missy, my student-slash-worker-slash-slave, slid to a stop when she saw Emily, nervously grabbing her brown ponytail and bringing it over her shoulder to fiddle with. Missy was training with me to work her way up the levels while she helped me manage my barn. Her brown eyes got wide as she took in the two of us.

I stopped cleaning and turned to Emily with a frown.

"You blocked in the transport truck? Really?" Okay, enough was enough. "Emily, I have clients due here in an hour for a lesson. Abigail has made her decision and yelling at me does nothing but make you look bad. And driving an hour and a half out of San Francisco to Barrow Bay, California, is even worse. I didn't go out to steal your client. Your scores were slipping. Your last few shows were unimpressive. You had to see this coming. Abigail said she would tell you this was coming."

In fact, Abby had assured me she would deal with breaking the news to Emily herself, but I had to admit this wouldn't be the first time that a client avoided confrontation by 'forgetting' to tell the old trainer. In hindsight, I don't know why I thought Abby would be any different. I sighed. "I'm sorry if she didn't, but it isn't my fault, nor can I afford to turn down clients

because you under-performed on your best horse."
Oops. That last part was supposed to be trying for
conciliatory. I would have to work on that later.

"Under-performed? UNDER-PERFORMED? You
don't know what you're talking about. I put in years of
strong performances, only to have her pull him after a
few bad scores. I'm going to be on the Olympic team
one day."

And yet I just put your only Olympic quality horse
in my barn... guess it would not be in the next few years.
Maybe the next one.

"Well, good luck with that, Emily." I shouldn't rub
it in about the horse. Self-control. "Let me show you out
so the transport truck can leave." I moved towards her,
copying her earlier move, only, unlike me, she gave
ground and moved towards the front of the barn. After
two backward steps, she turned and, with one final dirty
look, stalked towards the door.

"This isn't over! Everyone will know what you did!"

"Okay, bye! Have a nice drive home," I called out
after her with a friendly wave. "Shiitake Shrew." Well, at
least I waited until she was out of hearing to swear. Or
not-swear, as the case may be.

"Oh, Lark. You need to work on that potty mouth,"
Missy commented, with a shake of her head.

"Your sarcasm isn't appreciated. Also, have you
tried to find a replacement for the b-word? Nothing
works as well. It's unfortunate. And I'm not saying
'Beeyotch' or whatever it is people say now. Nope." I
shook my head at her. "And just you wait. One day you

will have a child who will parrot every bad word you say back to everyone they know, and I will laugh when you start using creative non-swear words, too."

"Please! I'm never having kids."

"Please!" I mocked. "You think when I was 18, I thought I would have kids? Or that I would actually have one at 23?" I snorted as I went to put Bon's halter where it was supposed to be and grabbed Twice. "Life doesn't consult you sometimes. Oh, and birth control can fail. Be prepared."

"Not really an issue right now," she answered with a grimace.

"I thought you went on a date last week."

"We went to the McDonalds in Misne. A McDonalds, Lark!" She shook her head as she grabbed a grooming tool to help me clean Twice. "He didn't even pay for everything. I'm done dating boys from the town. I'm going to go get me a city boy, like you did."

I winced at the reminder.

"I don't know if what we're doing counts as dating. We're just friends." When Detective Brecken of the San Francisco Police Department, also known as Captain America by those of us within the town, left the town after his case wrapped up — one that started with me getting body parts — I was elated for two days. Too elated. Two whole days of thinking we had chemistry. Two days to get my hopes up. Then two weeks of a few texts and even fewer calls left me disappointed and having several conversations with myself about how my expectations needed to be lower. Substantially. That didn't stop my hopes from rising every time I did get a text.

But after my last marriage, I was done being ignored by men, especially for their job, and Brecken was a workaholic. It didn't help that I couldn't argue against him working all the time since he was saving lives and solving crimes, both very important things. But I still felt ignored, or at least, not equally invested in our possible relationship. It didn't help that I felt like he was hiding something from me.

I had also found that communication mostly through text messages was difficult when my main communication style was sarcasm with a side of wit. It turned out, sarcasm did not come out right. At all. Then, when we did trade texts, I spent hours afterward trying to figure out what he meant. Dating wasn't for the weak. Or texting, for that matter. But my heart still wished he would suddenly be over the top, Hollywood-style infatuated. My anxiety was happy with our current speed. I was conflicted.

"At least he was hot. Could he kiss? Please tell me you kissed him?"

Ha! I knew better than to answer this question. Or, at least I did, now. When Jen, my best friend, asked, I told her the truth, which then led to two weeks of her bemoaning not knowing if he could kiss. Not knowing was a 'crime against women everywhere,' according to her. I, however, was pretty sure many women had sampled him in his 32 years. My lack of sampling wasn't affecting women-kind as a whole.

I lied when Gran asked, and said yes, but made the mistake of saying that he was a bad kisser. That went even worse. I didn't know *that* many articles have been written on how to teach a man to kiss.

"I'm sure your mother doesn't want me talking about my sex life, or lack of it, with you."

"Oh please. You just told me birth control fails. I think we're past that."

"I'm sure your mother supports anything that scares you into abstinence."

"It failed."

"I tried." I shrugged. I had done my best.

"I noticed you still didn't answer if he can kiss."

"That's because I'm not going to." I stuck my tongue out at her before I threw the saddle over Twice's back and attached the girth. "Jill will be here soon. Can you help her get tacked up for her lesson? Then you can go home for the day."

"Will do. Have a good ride, boss." She saluted me incorrectly, only using three fingers and her elbow dropped too low, before sauntering away.

"Don't call me 'boss'!" I called after her. "It makes me feel old."

"That's because you are!"

"I hate you! Why do I let you hang around here?"

"Because you hate clipping horses in the winter."

"Good point. Call me what you want." I would put up with just about anything to not have to body clip their hair or shave my horses. During the winter any sweat in the undercoat that didn't dry could make them sick. Removing the hair by shaving it like a hairy dog in summer was safer for the horse and easier for the rider, but horse hair had an amazing talent to get into places that should not be spoken of out loud. Anyone who had the option avoided shaving. Grabbing the mare's bridle, I slipped the bit into her mouth before leading her out. Time to put my training where my mouth was.

***

When I got home that night, my daughter, Hailey, greeted me at the door. I just finished saying goodnight to Gran when she jumped out at me.

"Can I go to Dad's this weekend?"

"Umm…" Could I get in the door before I had to make decisions? Hailey's wide, pleading eyes indicated no.

"There's another festival, like the one I went to with Dad and I want to go again. Jennie wanted to go and couldn't, so I got to tell everyone about it, and so I want to go again, because her parents said no, and—"

"Wait! Her parents said no? Why would they say no?" I was starting to have a sinking hunch I should have paid more attention to the festival the first time around.

"Because Jazz is the Devil's music."

"Ok, then." I needed to limit how much access Jennie's parents had to my child. "Yeah, I think—"

"And they had a major drug bust at the last one."

"What?!" I was going to kill my ex. "What do you mean they had a drug bust?"

"It was so cool! The cops came in and tackled this guy to the ground and then his friends got in on the act—" My hand swung up to stop her words. No. I didn't need any more information.

Killing wasn't good enough for him.

"I need to call your father." And my lawyer.

"You can't! I promised him I wouldn't tell you. You wouldn't make a liar out of me, would you?" She even gave me a quivering lower lip along with her puppy-dog eyes. It wouldn't have worked if I hadn't remembered the reason she was there in the first place: I had been getting body parts delivered to my door, thanks to our crazy ex-cafe owner, and couldn't bring her home until it was safe. *Fudge buckets.*

"No festival, but I won't tell your dad you told me, and you can go to his house Saturday. My final offer." Stupid divorce agreement. Why had I made the promise that I wouldn't stop her from seeing him if she wanted to?

"Moooom. That was your only offer." My child. Seven years old and already a smart aleck. I was so proud.

"Dinner! Then you can watch TV before bed." I moved past her to reach the kitchen, opening the refrigerator door and staring into the abyss looking for anything I might be able to mix together. Dinner... dinner... how bad of a parent was I if I gave her cereal?

"I have homework."

Huh? Oh. Yeah. Homework. Good for her.

"That's what I meant. You can watch TV after your homework." Why did they give seven-year-olds homework? How much did a seven-year-old need to learn? And why couldn't it be done during school hours, so all I had to do with her was the fun stuff? It seemed less like homework for her, and more forced parental engagement. I looked at the fridge again. I really was too tired to cook. "How do you feel about cereal for dinner?" She looked at me like she was eighty.

"I want carrots. And hummus. Oh! And tea."

"You spend too much time with your great-grandmother," I grumbled.

"I take that as a compliment." She sniffed and raised her nose in the air in a very familiar manner. Great. I was raising a more sarcastic version of Gran. Good luck, world.

"You say that now…" I muttered under my breath as I reached in and grabbed the hummus and carrots, sliding them over to her. So long as she was eating healthy, who was I to judge? I still grabbed the cereal, complete with marshmallows, and ate it, as my seven-year-old munched on carrots. Because I was an adult like that. "So how was school?"

"School."

Hmm. Usually my seven-year-old talked a lot.

Wait. I liked this version better. Maybe.

After a few seconds of silence, she threw me a bone. "How was work?"

"Got a new horse in training."

"The fancy one?"

"Yep."

"So, are you going to be doing a lot of shows this season?"

"The owner's plan is to throw him at every international level show we can, so yeah. You going to be okay with that?"

"Do I get to stay with Dad when you're gone?"

Not anymore, she didn't. Drug busts around my child. She'd only stay with him if it was my last choice. Or the divorce agreement made me. Which it did. *Fudge buckets*. Luckily, it wasn't often.

"Maybe. Depends on school. You don't mind staying with Gran, right?"

"Nope. Why did they ask you to show it?" Her earnest face took the sting out of the question, although it still smarted a little.

"Bon — that's the horse — had three really bad shows in a row at the end of last year. The owner felt that the trainer was having trouble unlocking the horse's true potential. Even stated that the horse seemed to regress starting about five months ago. So, she asked around about where I had moved and contacted me to see if I could do better."

"So, this is important?"

Yep. As in this could make or break my business, but I couldn't tell her that.

"A little. I know I can do what they want. I just have to find out why the horse isn't performing well." I smiled at her, covering my nerves. "How could I fail with such a great cheering section?"

She smiled back at me. "I know you'll be good."

"Thank you, Hailey Bailey." We beamed at each other before she frowned and looked down to the table where paper had gathered while I wasn't looking. It was like evil magic. One moment food, the next, homework.

"I still need help with my homework."

Ugh.

"Is it too late to get a different cheering section? There has to be one without homework."

"Mooom!"

"Fine, fine. Homework it is."

CHAPTER 2

"How was your ride?" Missy asked as she took Bon's reins from me. I frowned and sent another critical eye over him as I had several times since I rode him yesterday. He had been here four days, and I had yet to see the horse I thought he should be. I was starting to question my skills at this point, as much as it hurt to admit.

"Unimpressive. I mean, he has solid training, but there's no way he's at the level I was told. It's like they took a high school football star and sent him straight to professional sports. He's missing something." Like the impressive shoulder movement and impulsion. I wasn't really sure where he could hide something like that. I stroked his nose as I studied him, letting him lean into the scratch, moving my hand to the perfect place. Yep. He still looked fine.

"One — you know that comparison doesn't work very well, right? They used to do that all the time."

I glared. So, I didn't follow other sports. *Sue me.*

"Two — what's missing in that comparison is experience. But, that doesn't make any sense. Bon has been actively competing for years." She joined me in staring at the gelding like he would talk and tell us what the problem was.

He didn't.

"Exactly. He spent all of last year chasing the scores to bump him into the top level and yet the horse I sat on feels a whole level down from that. A whole level lower than he was competing in *last* year. So far this horse is a high school superstar failing in the Pro world." And I had no idea how to fix it.

"Doesn't the client expect him to try for the Olympic trials next year? Maybe go to Europe and do a few shows over there?"

"Yep." Not that I was excited about leaving Hailey with her dad for that long.

"Can you get him there?"

"Nope. But I'll try anyway." Money talks and the desperation to make my business work was a huge driver. "I don't get it. I saw him going last year. The horse I saw was everything Abby thinks he is. Maybe he's hurting somewhere that isn't obvious? I checked him over thoroughly this morning and after yesterday's ride looking for anything that might indicate a problem, but nothing. Did the owner tell us what supplements he was—"

"I can help with that." A male voice came from behind us, making me jump and spin to face the intruder. Bon, bless his little heart, didn't react to either the noise or my antics. Which made me frown. He got spooked twice at a fence post during the ride, but me jumping and spinning was fine. Weird animal. I pulled my eyes off the horse to take in the newcomer.

"Hi! Can I help you?" I managed a professional tone despite the hand on my chest trying to calm my racing heart.

"Hey. I'm Connor Willis. Bon's veterinarian."

"Oh. Yes. I know Abby mentioned you, but I didn't know you were coming out today." Or that he was under thirty-five, handsome, and really, really tall. I was not a short girl and I was still craning my neck up to meet his gaze. Poor Missy must be getting a crick in her neck looking. His golden eyes and brown hair were nice enough, but it was his smile that really made me pause. Mostly because it made me smile back. Sighing, I forced down my envy of people who had a contagious smile, which was difficult since this man had a smile that could stop traffic. All information that would be good to know before I was hit by it and taken off my game. It also explained why Abby was using a relatively new vet that no one was familiar with. Abby's eye for a tidy rear was well-known.

"I was in the area and thought I would stop by."

Really? Why was a vet, whose clients, I assume, were all in the city, an hour and a half out? I knew he had joined an existing practice, but I didn't know much more about how he was doing, mostly because I liked my vet and had no interest in any other.

He kept going before I could ask. "Abby mentioned that she moved him out here when we spoke yesterday; I wanted to make sure that he was okay from the transfer, and I didn't have your number." His smile grew a little, and he stepped into my space, to take a good look at Bon while I tried to decide if he was too close or if it was okay so long as he kept smiling at me. Wait! Oh, lord. I need to forget that last part. Too close. He was too close. And smelled too good. Like he just showered before coming here, crisp with a hint of mint. I took a step back, out of smelling distance, and focused.

"He seems good. I've been keeping an eye on him and my vet stopped by and glanced him over yesterday. Said there was nothing he could see." This made Connor's face fall, and I realized I might have insulted him. "Not that we wouldn't call you. My vet was just here... so he looked... and was willing to do it to relieve my mind. Really, it was an impulse thing since he was here." I hated hurting people's feelings. Probably why horse training worked so well for me. The only animal I had to be firm with had four legs and couldn't talk back. Well, they could, but I knew what the answer was. I was relieved when the hurt expression left his face and the smile returned.

"No, no. That was nice of him. You are taking great care of Bon." He reached out to touch my shoulder for a second — trying to reassure me? — then turned back to Bon. "Mind if I look him over myself?" He gestured to the horse, and I jumped out of the way.

"No, go right ahead." Smooth, Lark, smooth. Nice to know I still completely lost my cool around attractive guys. I swore 'they' promised it would go away at some point. I would be cool as a cucumber no matter who was talking to me. So far, I was batting a zero. Goodness knows my ex wouldn't have gotten away with half his behavior if I wasn't too busy looking into his eyes to pay attention to what he was doing. Then again, after Blake, it had been until Brecken for me to notice another man, so maybe I should blame him. Either of the hims. I grabbed Missy, and we both took something as an excuse to walk into the side room where I kept the tack.

"He's hot!" Missy hissed under her breath.

"Do people your age even use that word anymore?"

"Of course. It's a good descriptor. Matches when I say he's delicious and that I would like to take a bite out of that."

God save me from hormonal 18-year-olds.

"He's my age! Too old for you. Find someone in your generation."

"Technically we're all Millennials."

"No! Seriously? Dang. That makes me feel young *and* old at the same time." No, I was not accepting that I was in the same generation as people who are just starting to drive. Pulling out my phone, I googled it. "Ha! Nope. It ends with 22-year-olds. Your generation doesn't have a name yet!" I still felt jaded and old, but not as bad.

"Okay. Fine. He's too old for me. But he's the right age for you."

Oh, no. I needed to cut this in the bud right now.

"Why does everyone think I need a man? I'm happy all by myself. I have my daughter and my horses and… and my job and…" Think, Lark, think. "… and my family! I'm fine." Okay, maybe I needed a few more hobbies in my life, but I didn't need a man.

"Do I even need to tell you how pathetic that sounded? You just listed your life. Only unhappy people list their lives."

"Missy. You are 18. You are supposed to be stupid and awkward, not quick and sarcastic. Please act your age."

"My age is boring."

True. Life had gotten a lot more interesting once I could drink, but I couldn't tell her that.

"What are you talking about? College is fun. Lots about college is fun." Drinking? No, no advocating underage drinking. Sex was not where this conversation was supposed to go, either. My brain fumbled for an answer. "College boys!" Oops. We were supposed to not be mentioning sex. "Only having night classes!" This would have been easier to sell if I had actually gone to college. My sales pitch was lacking, even to me, and Missy rolled her eyes grabbing Twice's saddle. Yep. I hadn't sold it. I hoped I could get it better before Haley was her age.

"Lark?" Jen's voice echoed down the barn. Wow. I hadn't had this many visitors in, well, forever. Missy and I left the tack room to walk to the front of the barn to meet her.

"Hey, Jen! What are you doing out here?"

Jen, my best friend who worked out of her house as a CPA and business consultant, lived close to me in town. My barn, on the other hand, was all the way on the outskirts of town.

"I needed to get away from my house." Her eyes were dull and her dyed blonde hair was in a messy bun, instead of her normal neat ponytail. Not good at all.

"What happened?" I demanded, dropping everything to address this.

"Nothing."

"Yeah… that was believable." I didn't even try to hide my sarcasm.

"Nothing I can talk about. Just distract me." She gazed at me like I was going to start dancing at her command.

Hmm. Dancing I was a little out of touch with right now, but… "I have a hot vet. You want him?"

"You're giving away men now? Because if so, can I have Captain America? Unless you found a real-life Iron Man, because a girl has to have favorites." It did pick her up a little, even if she was more excited about my man than the vet.

Wait. Not my man. Not anyone's man. My friend-like person. Who was hot. Like, movie star, just-walked-off-the-set-of-a-movie hot. Blond hair, blue eyes, he was one longer nose away from looking exactly like Chris Evans, the star that played Captain America. And, much to his embarrassment and our joy, the nickname stuck.

"I think Thor was the hottest, personally," Missy added. Jen and I both looked at each other and shook our heads.

"Please. Who cares about hot? Rich, smart, and funny. That's what I want in a man," Jen told Missy, sighing at the thought. They both then turned to me.

"What?"

"Aren't you going to defend Captain America?" Missy demanded.

"Why? Because he looks like Brecken? Or, I guess it would be Brecken who looks like him? No. I'm not getting into this. I'm a single mother with a career and her own business. No man needed."

"That's the second time she has had to remind herself she's an independent lady. And that she has a good life," Missy pointed out to Jen.

"Seriously! Less smart and observant! Go look up what normal 18-year-olds are like." I shot her a scowl and moved back towards the cross ties before I remembered that Connor was using them for his inspection and stopped at the door, not knowing where to go. Escape fail.

"Yep. Definitely trying too hard. I think she misses Brecken," Jen said as she followed.

"NO! I do not miss what I didn't have. I'm a single woman and happy to be."

"I thought you guys were *thinking* about dating," Missy asked. Or maybe mocked. There probably was some mocking in there. My issues with dating and relationships had brought me to some ridiculous lengths.

"Nope. I'm single. Footloose and fancy free. Not tied down. Free to mingle. Whatever you want to call it." And we were talking about talking. Which was too ridiculous to say out loud.

"Well, I'm happy to hear that."

Oh no. My eyes slid closed for a second as I hoped that I had imagined Connor's voice behind me.

"Well, hello. You must be the new vet." I could hear the glee in Jen's voice. Maybe if I was still enough they would forget I was here.

"Yep. Connor Willis. I just moved here from Washington State." I felt him move past me to shake her hand, and then come back to stand beside me. "Is there a point where she opens her eyes again? They're much too pretty to stay hidden behind her lids."

My eyes flew open. The new vet *was* flirting with me. Badly, but I had to admit his smile made up for it. What was I supposed to do? Flirt back? *Could* I flirt back? He was a client's vet. Was there some rule about this? God, this was so much easier when I was married and had to say no. I knew the answer then. I wasn't so sure now. Would Brecken want me to say no? Should I care what Brecken wanted?

"No… I mean yes. To the open eyes thing. I'm fine. Just embarrassed that you caught me being so unprofessional. I try to save my weird for when people have known me more than twenty minutes." He smiled at my joke and, like clockwork, I ended up smiling back. He *was* cute. I guessed a little flirting wouldn't hurt. "So why did you move here from Washington?"

"I needed a break from all the rain. Got an offer with a friend of mine to move in with him in the city and do the equine section of his practice, so I moved. Been here about a year. Been slowly building up my clients."

Interesting. In my experience vets didn't travel around much once they set up their practice since horse people were notorious for being slow to trust new people with their beloved pet's health. Good for him for being willing to try a new location.

"Do you miss Washington?" I asked. I had thought about moving up there for a half a second after the divorce. Before Gran got her hooks into me.

"Nope. Washington and I didn't really agree. I've been doing much better down here." He flashed another smile, and we all returned it.

"Well, I'm glad I got to meet you today. I'm sorry that I moved before you came to town. I moved here about two years ago, after my divorce. Do you have many clients out this way?" In other words, how hard would it be to get his attention? I was guessing from the flirting he was single, but clients could be even more demanding than significant others sometimes.

"A few. We should see each other pretty regularly." He glanced at his truck for a second before turning back to me. "Since I'll be in Barrow Bay more often with Bon out this way, maybe next time I'm out you can show me around the town?"

Why not?

"Sure. Let me know when you're coming back out and I'll clear my schedule."

Jen and Missy's eyes bulged a little, but both gave me a thumbs-up sign. See? I didn't need Brecken. There were other, less busy fish in this sea. "Shall I walk you to the car? I have some questions about Bon's history." Connor smiled and gestured for me to go first. We slipped past Jen and Missy, who were both wearing annoyingly cheesy smiles. Brats.

I waited until we were out of the barn to speak.

"Hey, I don't know how close you were with Emily, but I was wondering if you could answer some questions for me. Bon doesn't seem to be moving with the same level of freedom I saw a few months ago at the show, and I know Abby moved him because of performance issues. Did Abby talk to you about anything?"

His eyes got wide and a little of the color in his face drained before he composed himself again. Did he think I was trying to undermine him? I didn't mean to. I wouldn't ever try to get a client to switch vets. Wow. I'd known this man for twenty minutes and managed to insult him twice. Go me.

"No. Abby didn't say anything. Do you want to do some testing?"

"I don't really know where to start. He doesn't have any tender spots or swelling. We looked everywhere for something. If you asked me, I would tell you he's a perfectly healthy horse. But he isn't moving the same."

"Maybe it's the location. He might still need some time to adjust to the new barn and rider. Why don't we wait a few days and then talk again next week?" He took my hands and patted the top one, using his golden eyes to stare into mine with conviction. I was evidently a sucker for brown eyes and dark lashes. I might need to find more self-control if this continued.

"I can't wait until the next time we see each other," he continued. "Let me know if you have any reason for me to come out. Here's my card. Call anytime."

"I will." Oh, god. That came out in a sigh. I needed to have some self-respect!

"Good! I'll be seeing you soon." I stood there as he got in his truck and drove away, still a little dazed from the flirting. As I added his contacts to my phone, connecting them with Abby's info, I noticed Jen and Missy watching from the door to the barn. Well, I'd procrastinated long enough. Time to pay the piper and go answer their questions.

Ding.

I looked down at my phone and saw that Lindsey's town blog had a new article. Lindsey had taken over the void when our local paper closed by starting a blog for local news. Unlike a traditional newspaper, Lindsey didn't have anyone to tell her no, so our news was now less impartial and more, well, gossip. For a second, I hesitated.

No. That was silly. There was no way it could be about me... "*Lark Finds a New Man.*"

Son of a biscuit.

"Which one of you two blabbed? Out with it! Or you both die!" I growled at them as I stalked toward them, waving my phone in front of me. Both looked alarmed and Missy turned to go back in the barn.

"I have horses to get ready and chores to do, like getting Twice tacked up for your ride. So you remember why you let me ride your school master, Bob." My old show horse was helping Missy go up the levels and get her dressage scores.

I sighed, realizing that having Bon and Bob in the same barn was going to get confusing. Maybe Bon could be blessed with a new nickname.

"And show him!" I reminded her as she went in. "So don't forget who you are loyal to." She waved acknowledgment as she rushed to Twice's stall, earning her an annoyed glance from the mare. Jen opened her mouth, but I held up my hand to hold her off as I watched. Missy, forgetting the contrary nature of the mare in her hurry to get away from me, was rushing to get the halter on and Twice saw the opening. I waited until Twice was committed for the bite before I interceded. "Twice!" Both heads came swinging up to find me, one with wide questioning eyes and one with a glare that begrudgingly admitted she didn't want to get into it today. Smart mare.

Assured that the mare knew her place, I turned to Jen and frowned.

"I didn't tell her," she protested.

"Et tu, Brutus?"

"One, it's 'et tu, brute.' If you are going to quote Shakespeare, get it right. Two, I didn't tell Lindsey."

I stared, not believing her for a second. Missy would never out me. At least not that quickly. If Missy had told on me, she would have texted her friends who would then tell their parents, who would eventually say something where Lindsey could hear. That would take two hours, at least.

Finally, Jen broke. "Buuut, I might have texted your Grandmother."

"Who's at Bingo Brunch this morning."

"Who *is* at Bingo Brunch this morning," she conceded, fighting off a grin.

"With Lindsey."

"Yeah, I kind of forgot that. Sorry." Her eyes met mine and I could see some regret. Behind the amusement.

Sigh. Damage was done. I was going to have to let this one go.

"I haven't read it yet. Should I?"

She winced, and I knew her answer without needing to be told. "Okay, we're going out tonight and you are buying me a drink." As I opened my phone, I caught a glance at the number of comments after the article. "Maybe three."

God save me from this town.

CHAPTER 3

Jen hung around the barn all day, laughing as Twice tried to run away bucking, the mare expressing her dislike of my opinions. She also cheered as Missy got repetitive flying lead changes on Bob for the first time, making him look like he was skipping down the arena. She only started to get antsy when we were putting away the last horse.

It was a little past three and Missy had gone home to get ready for her classes at the community college. Jen made the mistake of getting her phone out of her car while she waited for me to finish. Four text messages later she was back to twirling her dyed blond hair between her fingers only to drop it and go to chewing on her thumb. Then back again.

Something was seriously wrong, but I knew it was related to work and she wasn't about to tell me anything. No, today I wasn't the confidant. I was the distraction. I took another look, watching as she spit out a chunk of nail she had ripped off her thumb, before I grabbed my phone. This required a big distraction. And a nail salon.

Me: *Hey Gran! Can you watch Hailey tonight? Jen's having a really bad day, and I was going to go buy her a few drinks.*

Gran: *Did you say yes to the cute vet?*

Sigh.

Me: *Yes. Next time he's out I promised to show him the town. Happy?*

Gran: *What about Brecken?*

Maybe Hailey could come drinking with us. She's seven. Maybe that's old enough.

Me: *What about him?*

Gran: *He isn't going to like you going on dates with other men.*

Me: *Then he needs to talk to me. Hailey?*

Gran: *Sure. Go. Have fun. Call Brecken and see if he can meet you. Or you and Jen could go to him!*

Me: *No. He isn't interested. Give it up, Gran.*

Gran: *He'll come around, sweetie.*

Now I was moping because of a man. Glad Gran let me know, I would hate to act happy when the town has me depressed.

"Okay, Jen. Let's head to a bar. We have drinking to do." I grabbed her hand, and we got in my truck, leaving Jen's car at the barn. It would be easy enough to grab her tomorrow morning to come back and pick it up after yoga. Plus, maybe I could talk her into doughnuts. She sat down with a long sigh and stared out the front window with a blank stare. I let her be while I got the truck going, waiting for her to break the silence. When nothing happened, I reached for something to say.

"Mind if I stop by my house to change into something less… skin tight?" I frowned when that only elicited a nod and what I was pretty sure was a wave from her hand. I drove back to my house, glancing at her in between staring at the road, but not knowing how to break the ice. I hadn't come up with anything as we pulled in and I parked. Letting a long breath out, I went with the obvious.

"Want to come in?"

"No. I think I'll stay here." She turned away from me and kept her gaze locked on something outside of the car. Still short of the inspirational uplifting comment that best friends were supposed to have in these moments, I quietly got out of the truck and slipped into the house to change into jeans and a shirt. She hadn't moved when I got back, but I was done waiting for her. Well, I would've been if I knew where to start. She seemed to be ignoring my staring, but finally she caved.

"I think I have a problem," she admitted to the passenger window.

"Work, relationships, or family?"

"Work." Jen sighed, keeping her gaze on the scenery, but I had a feeling she wasn't seeing any of it.

"Do you want to talk about it?"

"Can't." Alright then. I turned the truck back on and pulled out of my driveway.

"The Pub work for you?"

"Sure."

Uh oh. She didn't make fun of my pizza habit. This was DEFCON six. Or one? I could never keep those straight. Either way, the best friend pressure was on and I was falling short. Maybe if I gave her enough alcohol, she'd forget my lack of ability to make her feel better. Or was I supposed to make her talk her feelings out? Nah. Denial helped me through the divorce. It could work for her, too. I hoped. We sat in silence as I drove to the bar, but Jen broke again when I parked. Maybe my awkward glances worked.

"It's a client. I..." She bit her lips together and looked away again.

I struggled between wanting to know the whole story and respecting her job.

"Did you make a mistake, or did they?"

"He did. In coming to me." She swung open the door, not glancing back to see if I was following. Guess we were done with the confessions portion of this evening. I rapidly released my seat belt to follow. I caught up quickly, and together we headed into The Pub, claiming a table on the far side of the bar. The Pub wasn't too busy tonight, with only a few people sitting up at the bar. Guess not a lot of people were drinking on a Thursday. I enjoyed off-season at the resort. So much more room to breathe.

The town was supported by the business our local resort brought in, and during the summer months it was full to the brim with the rich, the richer, and those lucky few who got to pretend to be rich for a few days. Being that we were in California, the resort did a pretty decent business year round, but the winter months were more manageable.

Becky, an energetic brunette with a penchant for dangling earrings and bad boys, was working tonight, and she nodded at me, lifting a finger to tell me she would be over in a second.

"So, how's dating going?" I asked. That was usually a good conversation starter.

"Men suck. Romance sucks. Do you think if I try hard enough, I can become a lesbian?" She let out a large, melodramatic sigh that almost make me smile, but I held it back. Smiling would be bad.

"That's not how it works."

"Damn it."

When Becky came over, we placed our order and then I dug into the only topic she seemed to be willing to talk about. Kind of.

"What brought on this new hatred of all things men?"

"Nothing, I guess." She sighed, studying the table in front of her as she looked for the right words. "I've been focused on other things, and men, well, they've been too much effort."

She gave me a short smile at the end, to tell me she was okay, but it fell off her face too quickly.

"Oh my god." Her eyes went wide, and she froze, focused on something by the door. When her eyes only got wider as she turned back, I knew whatever the issue was, it wasn't going to be good and it probably had something to do with me.

To look, or not to look. That was the question.

"Lark?" A low voice came from behind me. A low voice that I had been trying to forget.

Fudge buckets. There was no way that he… on today, of all days? *Fudge buckets filled with shiitake mushrooms.*

"Brecken?" I caved to the inevitable and turned to face him.

"I, umm… I got a few days off from work, so I thought… No. This was a bad idea. It's wrong. This isn't the way this should go. No, I should go." He nodded to himself and turned away from me, moving as if he was going to leave.

"That's it?" I was strangely calm. Like, what-is-wrong-with-me calm. Plus, what about this was a bad idea? Was I a bad idea? Was surprising me a bad idea? Because that one actually was; I didn't like surprises. I was the girl that tended to kick people who jumped out at me.

He had started to walk away after his lame comment, but my words stopped him.

"What do you mean?" he asked as he turned back to face me.

"A few texts and you just show up? What are you expecting?" My tone was even, and I was surprised to feel only curiosity. Maybe getting asked out today had put some perspective on my non-relationship with Brecken. Maybe I was too angry that he wasn't in the same place as I was, and it was making me numb. Who knew?

"I wasn't expecting anything." He shifted from one foot to the other as I watched. "I have a room at the resort. I thought it might be nice to come see you."

Okay. I didn't know what to do with that. I mean, there had been no promises, so I couldn't be angry that he kind of disappeared into his job the minute he got back to the city. Unfortunately for him, my emotions didn't listen to my logic. They had decided that was the wrong answer and were stirring for a fight.

Or write it off as beginning dating stuff and start intense flirting. My emotions were completely undecided.

"Well, it's nice to see you, I guess. What—" My words were cut off by my phone, which was buzzing in my pocket.

I held my hand out while I pulled out my phone and glanced at the caller ID. It was Billy, my stall cleaner and feeder. "Billy?" I couldn't help my short tone. Billy didn't call unless there was a problem. I was lucky to have found him when I moved here. He had been a groom at a professional barn back in the city, and when his old trainer heard I was moving to town, she sent me his contact information. He hadn't wanted to get back into grooming, as he took care of his kids during the day, but he was more than interested in feeding and cleaning and he really knew his stuff.

"Your new horse isn't eating." His voice was abrupt, not even bothering with a greeting.

And cue the adrenaline.

"Billy, can you get him out and walk him? I'm about fifteen minutes away." I started to gather my stuff and shifted towards the edge of the seat. Well, I grabbed my purse and keys. That's stuff.

"Will do."

I hung up and got out, slipping past Brecken and rushing towards the door. Flirting would have to wait. Or yelling. Whatever I had been about to do.

"I have to go. I have an issue at the barn. I'll talk with you guys later," I called over my shoulder to Jen and Brecken, who both looked slightly surprised.

I stopped for a second, debating calling my own vet instead of Connor. It was tempting, but the client was always right. Being the responsible trainer meant using the people the client wanted me to use. Unless Connor didn't answer. Then I was free to call in whoever could get here the quickest.

Calling Connor, I slipped into my truck holding my breath as I waited for the phone to ring. The small part of me that hoped that he wouldn't answer made me freeze as the phone rang a third time. Maybe I would be able to call my own vet, who could be at the barn in a half hour, but on the fourth ring I was unlucky. Or lucky, I guessed, as Connor was supposed to be the preferred vet. As I pulled the truck into reverse, I listened for Connor's answer.

"Hello? This is Connor." His tone gave me the impression that he thought I was calling for personal reasons.

Sorry to burst that bubble, buddy.

"Hey Connor, it's Lark. We might have an issue with Bon. How far out are you?"

"I can be there in an hour." His tone was no longer happy.

"Okay. I'm on my way back to the barn right now. I saw him about…" I looked at the clock and calculated when the last time I looked into his stall was. "…an hour ago, and he looked fine, but my feeder says he isn't eating. You want me to call you when I get there?"

"Yes. I'm jumping in my truck now."

"Okay. I'll let you know if we're going to head to the equine hospital immediately."

"Got it. Talk with you soon."

I dropped the phone, letting him end the call, and focused on getting to the barn as fast as possible.

There could be lots of reasons that a horse didn't eat. Stress. Ulcers. They didn't feel like it today. But the most common reason was what scared me. A horse owner's worst nightmare. The 'C' word. Colic. It was a magical, mystical issue that stemmed from a horse's inability to throw up. As revolting and smelly as throwing up could be, turned out it was the difference between a resilient, thriving animal like humans, and horses, who were delicate little creatures that literally could die from a stomach ache.

I knew there were many reasons horses were not at the top of any food chain. No hands or thumbs, probably being one of the biggest, but in my mind, I liked to think it was deadly stomach aches that kept them at the bottom. It made me feel like at least there was a logic behind this horrible biological failure. Like it was a failure in all prey animals, that allowed predators to thrive. It wasn't, but I liked to think it was.

When I finally got to the barn, I flew out, barely getting the truck turned off before meeting Billy at the door of the barn.

"He was biting at his stomach."

Jesus, Joseph and Mary.

"Okay. Have you been walking him?"

"Yeah." He led me to Bon, who was standing in the middle of the stall, probably right where Billy had left him when he was put away. His food was in his feeder, untouched. I watched for a second, noticing that Bon hadn't acknowledged my presence or looked at the food.

Definitely colic. *Snickerdoodles.*

He wasn't thrashing on the ground, though. Or pawing.

Maybe it was just a light colic? There was no harm in thinking positively.

"Can you stay here? I'm going to go get some medication." I ran for my fridge, ignoring Bob's nicker and Twice's evil-eye. Reaching it, I grabbed some Banamine medication I had for colic emergencies and a syringe. Rushing back, I opened the stall door and had Billy follow me with a halter. "Can you hold him while I give him this? Then you can go. The vet is on his way."

He nodded and went to the opposite side of the horse, which was not the way I normally would have done it but I had learned soon after I had come here that Billy was not a big fan of needles. Seeing one made him pass out, so we all made a point to make him not see one. Ever. Hitting Bon's neck three times, then slipping the needle in on the third hit, I pushed the medication into his system. Pulling the needle out, I reached down to check his pulse before exiting the stall with Billy behind me.

"How is he?" Billy asked.

"His pulse is a little elevated, but not horrible. As long as he's standing quiet, it's better that he's in his stall, but I'm going to keep an eye on him. Go. You're already late, and your wife is going to be worried." He nodded and left, me listening for his truck as I called Bon's owner.

"Abby? It's Lark."

"What's wrong?" Her voice turned stressed.

Guess I was not the only one who got short when they received surprise calls.

"Bon seems to be colicing. I have already called Connor, and he's on his way out here. I wanted permission to take him to the hospital, if we need to."

"Oh no. Is he going to be ok?" Abby's voice was concerned and slightly panicked so I tried to be reassuring while making it clear that this was not a good situation.

"He seems to be doing okay right now, but I'll be keeping an eye on him until Connor gets here. He was biting his stomach earlier and not eating, so I'm thinking there's a strong possibility we'll be heading to the hospital tonight, even if it's just in case. With an insurance policy like his, I like to be on the safe side. Do I have your approval?"

"Yes. Do what you need to."

"Perfect. I'll text you as I know more." I hung up and went to my next call.

"Connor?"

"I'm still on my way. How is he?" Connor's voice was troubled and distracted, probably from driving.

"Not bad enough to take to the hospital now, but we might need to for the insurance policy. I gave him some medication. He isn't eating and his pulse is elevated, but he's standing quietly right now. I'll start walking him if that changes."

"Great. I'll be there soon. Call if he gets worse. Don't take him to the hospital until I see him." He hung up, and I stood there staring at the phone and then the horse. Bon stood still, still not moving, but this time he raised his head to meet my gaze. After a second, he stretched his head out, reaching to nuzzle my hand and I moved closer to him, stroking his nose as he snuggled his head into my arms.

He was definitely doing better. But, in all honesty, I didn't know why I questioned whether to go to the hospital or not. I was stupid. We were going even if Bon started eating and passing food again. I had to make sure that he was healthy, with no room for error. What if he got better and then worse again? Nope. With a horse like Bon, we needed to take him where he could be supervised during the night.

On the other hand, it would make me feel better to make sure the worst was passed before I put him, unsupervised, in the trailer. Maybe waiting for Connor wasn't a bad idea.

"Well, it's too late now. I guess we'll wait for him," I told Bon, as I snuggled his head closer to me, trying to give him what comfort I could.

We stood there for a while, me telling him all about my past, how I had met Brecken when he came here to investigate his missing cousin, who quickly turned up dead. Bon got a little restless at that point, so I walked him around the arena while I spilled more about my feelings on Brecken, and dating, and my general confusion about both.

By the time Connor got there, Bon knew more about me than Jen did, since he just listened and didn't point out when my logic wasn't, well, logical. Horses are great therapy for letting you process and reflect on your emotions. Too bad traditional therapy was cheaper.

We both heard Connor's truck pulling into the driveway. By this point, Bon was looking significantly better, and I wished that I had asked Billy to remove Bon's food before he left. Bon would be enjoying the post colic diet for a while after this scare. We both walked to meet Connor at the cross-ties so that Bon could get a thorough inspection.

Bon stood there, trying to get my attention and demand more snuggles, so I took a moment to do another assessment. He hadn't passed any waste, but the pained look was gone from his eyes and he had started to walk actively instead of being coaxed along. I thought we were clear but I wasn't the expert, and I couldn't shake the need to be on the side of too much caution. Especially with other people's horses.

"Lark. How's our boy doing?" Connor smiled as he walked in, and I flashed him a look of irritation before I caught myself. He had made good time. Smiling was probably just a polite reflex.

"Really good. He seems to be in less distress, but I haven't tried feeding him anything."

"Great. Great. Let me look him over and we'll make the call to take him to the hospital or not."

I stepped aside and he gave me another smile as he passed, which I weakly returned. This caused him to stop and put his hands on my shoulders, pulling my gaze to his. "Don't worry. I'm sure everything will be fine. You are a wonderful trainer."

I watched, hovering over his shoulder until he stood up, facing me as he snapped off his gloves.

"Well, he looks like he's doing ok, but it's still questionable enough that I would like to take him to the hospital for the night. Can you get his shipping boots so we can protect his legs in transport?"

At my nod, he went to his truck with his equipment. It took me a few minutes to find the boots which had been buried behind his other stuff, even in the few days he had been here.

I needed to talk to Missy about organizing this place better. We all knew I wasn't going to organize it.

When I made it back to Bon, Connor was walking back from his truck, wiping his hands off with a towel I didn't remember seeing earlier. Then again, if he was wiping off his hands, we must be ready to go.

"Do you want me to put the boots on while you hook up the trailer?" He reached for the boots, and I pulled back, holding the boots away from him.

"No. It's okay. I would feel better if I did it." I smiled to take the sting out of my words, but I needed the control of making sure the shipper boots were on correctly. Or, more specifically, I needed control over something and all I had were the shipper boots. Not that he would do them wrong, but I had a lot more experience. His lips thinned out at my refusal, but it was quickly replaced by another smile. They were starting to get annoying. Was he too happy? Was that even a thing?

"That's great. I'll take my truck and follow you to the hospital. The closest one is Hidden Creek, right? That's what's on the paperwork."

"Yep. Go right ahead. I'll follow you in a second." I watched him leave and then went to work putting on the boots. Finishing, I reached up to pat Bon's neck.

Eww. Why was my hand wet? I looked closer. There was a wet section, right where a shot would have been delivered. Puzzled, I thought back to when I gave him his shot. I was pretty sure that I had been on the other side. Plus, the alcohol I used to clean the location would have dried by now. Why did he have a new one? Had Connor given him a shot while I was getting the boots?

"Lark! You coming? I called Abby, and she's on her way to the hospital."

Shiitake mushrooms. I forgot about the wet spot and ran for the trailer. It took me about ten minutes to get it hooked up and another ten to get him loaded. Finally, we were underway. Abby had left me a text message asking me to call so I dialed as I pulled out, even though I knew she had been in contact with Connor already.

"Hey, Abby."

"You're going to the hospital?"

"Yes. It's better to be safe than sorry. He was doing much better when we put him in the trailer, though."

"Okay. I'll meet you there, then."

"See you soon." Good thing I hadn't gotten to drinking as it was an hour drive to the hospital. All I had to focus on was the dark road in front of me and getting there as quickly as possible so Connor could make sure Bon was okay. We could make it.

CHAPTER 4

We didn't make it. Well, I made it to the hospital, but when we opened the doors, Bon Voyage was dead. I let the experts past me, trying to figure out what I had missed. He was getting better when we left the barn. I could have sworn that this was just a precaution, not a life-or-death situation. Why was he dead on my trailer floor?

Connor had rushed in with the other vets, and now that they knew there was nothing to do, he had come back to my side, throwing an arm around me and giving me a small hug.

"There was nothing we could have done. He must have twisted a gut."

I glanced at him, willing to admit it was possible, but still unconvinced he would have gone down so quickly. I had been a trainer for a long time at this point, and this was fast. Too fast. He gave me another hug, probably reading the emotions on my face.

"What happens next?"

"I'll do a necropsy to confirm the cause of death. I promise I'll find out what happened. You didn't do anything wrong, Lark." He looked down at me with such conviction in his eyes that I believed him. For half a second, before my guilt came back.

"I had to have done something wrong. Missed some sign. He was doing so well when we put him in the trailer!" I buried my head in my hands for a second before he forced them down, using one of his own hands to bring my eyes to meet his. I felt a twinge of guilt that I had doubted him, too. Maybe if I hadn't been so hesitant around Connor, we would have been faster, and Bon could have gotten the help he needed.

Oblivious of my concerns, Connor kept trying to comfort me.

"I checked him over thoroughly. This was a precaution, just in case something happened. We got hit with the exception and not the rule. Even if we had been closer, he probably wouldn't have made it. Don't blame yourself." His hand came up to wipe away a tear from my cheek I hadn't noticed escaping. He then took both my hands in his, leading me away from the trailer. "I promise. I'll make his necropsy at the top of my list and I'll deliver the results to you in person." He held up my hands, wrapped in his and I nodded, comforted that he was on my side. "It wasn't your fault. These things happen."

I was going to need someone on my side. I let the heat of his hands center me as I took a deep breath.

What did I need to do next?

"I need coffee." Wait. I had their coffee before. I wasn't *that* stressed. "Never mind. I'm going to wait for

Abby in the waiting area while you guys work on removing… work on my trailer, if that's okay?"

"Go. I'll let you know when you can go home."

I nodded, heading to the waiting area to wait for Abby. I hadn't had to do many of these. Informing a client that their pride and joy had passed away. It was always hard. Telling Abby that the horse she brought over from Europe, had died within days of coming to my barn was going to be even harder.

I looked at my phone, debating what words I was going to use when I saw two missed calls from Jen, a text from Brecken, one call from Gran, and a notification that Lindsey had posted an article. Since I felt telling Abby was something I should do in person, I returned Gran's call first while I waited.

"Lark? Honey? Are you okay? Lindsey posted a blog that you ran out of the bar upset when Brecken showed up. I'm sorry that I didn't tell you he was coming. He didn't know for sure, so I didn't want to get your hopes up…"

Okay. Hold up.

There was so much there I was struggling to sort through all the manipulations.

"You knew? No, wait, Lindsey posted a blog saying that I ran out because… Oh… Fudge buckets." Too much. This was all too much. I couldn't handle this right now.

"He told me—"

"Wait! You're talking with Brecken? Why?" Never mind what I could or couldn't handle. We were starting there. Yep, that was a good place to start.

"I can have friends, too, young lady." Her tone was sharp. Definitely defensive. She was up to something.

"You can. Just not the men I'm talking with. Or not talking with, as the case may soon be." I couldn't believe he was talking to her more than me. So much for his whole 'you make me want to stay' bit. I hated men. Okay, maybe I wished I hated men. Or at least Brecken. Even a little bit.

"He needed some advice."

About what? About me?

Nope. Not getting sucked into that black hole again.

"No. No more. No being friends with men I'm talking with."

"That seems like an unfair rule." I could hear the pout in her voice, but I knew her enough to know it was only a manipulation.

Sigh. Time to get to the important topic.

"Gran, I had to take a horse to the hospital. I'm going to get back late tonight. Can you take Hailey overnight?" Sometimes I just had to roll with the crazy. I wasn't even going to ask about Lindsey's article.

"No problem, sweetie. You take care of that horse, and we'll be here when you get back." I debated telling her that the horse didn't make it, but I didn't trust my voice and I didn't want her to come running to my aid like she had when I was a little girl. Even if having someone to hug right now sounded pretty good. I hung up and moved on to answering Jen.

"Lark? You okay?"

"Not really."

"Oh no. Did one of your horses die?"

I swallowed hard, but nothing came out of my mouth in response. That seemed to be enough, though.

"I'm so sorry, babe. Well, then you take care of yourself and we'll talk about Brecken later," Jen continued.

"Or never. That's a good option, too." Really. I was definitely on Team Never.

"Please. You need to talk it out. You talk things out to process them."

Good point.

"Got an hour of processing while waiting for the vet. Bon…" Swallow. I could do this. I just had to keep talking. "Bon was a good listener. I'm good. No talking needed."

"Great. So, are you going to see him while he's here?"

Well. Wasn't that a good question. Was I up to seeing him? I tended to go a little weak in the knees and will power when around him. What if he was here for me? To make it work? I didn't know if I could do that. Or, even worse, what if he wasn't? Too much! I needed to ask.

"Why is he in town? I know he said he had some time, but, honestly, I don't know if I can handle being the reason right now."

"I think that it would be romantic if he was."

Ugg. Look at her being all healthy and normal. I glared at the phone.

"I don't know that I'm ready for romantic. I'm ready for taking it slow." Except for my emotions. They were expecting Hollywood insta-love with a side of romance. I was still working on getting my emotions and my head in the same place.

"Well, he definitely took it slow."

Sigh. "I don't want to talk about him right now. Okay? You can deal with my lack of answer tonight and I might call you tomorrow."

"I'm letting you off the hook tonight, but we're talking tomorrow."

"Not about Brecken." Please.

"Oh, I'm completely talking to you about Brecken. This only gets you a one-night pass. By the way, I picked up my car from your barn, so you don't need to worry about it."

Crazy. The whole town was crazy.

"Fine. But I'm not going to yoga. I'm sleeping in tomorrow."

"Sounds fair."

I hung up on her, shaking my head at her, but a laugh sitting inside me from her insane banter. But it, no, the whole town made me feel better. And their brand of crazy definitely made me feel loved.

Next was Brecken's text message. I let out a long breath before opening it. I really didn't know what I wanted it to say, and that scared me more than anything else.

Brecken: *You okay? You left in a hurry.*

Me: *One of my client's horses was colicing, and I had to take it to the hospital.*

Brecken: *Did he make it?*

Me: *No.*

Me: *I don't know what I did wrong.*

Brecken: *From my research, they colic easy. There might have been nothing you could do.*

He researched horses? Because I worked with them? For the first time since I got the call this evening I smiled, unable to hold back the warm giddiness in my chest. Maybe he wasn't as checked out as I thought he was.

"I don't think smiling is the reaction I want from a trainer that just lost my horse." A man came in the waiting room door, striding up to me with swift movements. I jumped to my feet in response, trying to remember if I had ever met Abby's husband before. This could be him, but I wasn't sure.

"Hello. My name is —"

"Larklyn Davis. You are the reject trainer my wife chose when she decided to move that money pit away from the city. Now he's dead, and you are the reason." He got even closer into my face and started waving his hands. "This is your fault."

Reject?

REJECT?!

My fault?

My anger clogged my throat for a moment before my professional persona took over. People who made a living serving others needed to be professional.

"I'm sorry for your loss, but I did everything I could to save your horse. I tried —"

"You didn't, or he would still be alive right now."

Low blow. Maybe breathing will help me stay calm. In. Out. Talk.

"Sir, I'm sure the necropsy will show —"

"Necropsy? What is that?" His anger was derailed by this new word, and I was fighting my fight-or-flight response as I was struggling to figure out what was worse. His curious face or his angry face.

"It's an autopsy, only when it's on an animal, we call it a necropsy," I explained.

"No. Unacceptable. There will be no necropsy. This is your fault, and you'll come forward to say it was. You'll accept full responsibility, or I'll tell everyone that you killed our horse. You'll never get a job in this town again!"

"That's not how it works." I was able to keep my voice even, but I could feel the sarcasm yearning to come out. Professional. Must stay professional. Maybe I should try counting? "The necropsy is done as a requirement of the insurance payout. So, I have nothing to do with it."

He didn't like that answer, his face turning red before he shuffled forward even more, causing his finger to dig into my chest. "No. You'll figure it out. No necropsy."

Done. I was done.

"I'll call the cops if you don't step back now." My voice was quiet, but there was a definite edge that told him I was serious. He took one step back before he regrouped and tried again.

"You'll claim responsibility, or I'll ruin you. You'll never work in this town again."

This town? Please.

"Sweet cheese and crackers! What part of middle of nowhere made you think I wanted to work in the San Francisco area in the first place? Threatening to ruin my reputation only works if I care, which I don't. So, take your threat and stuff it. I did everything I could to save that horse. I don't even know what went wrong. If you have a problem with your own insurance payout policies, take it up with them, but I did nothing wrong and I'll not lie to people because you need someone to blame. Now please get out of my face or I'll call the cops." Whew. I had to gasp for breath for a second, because spitting out all those words without stopping to breathe was hard. But for him, I was willing to do it.

Clap. Clap. Clap.

What the...?

I turned to see Abby entering in the doorway, clapping slowly. Oh, please don't let her have heard my complete break in professionalism.

"And that, dear husband, is why I picked Lark. You can't bully her. You can't push her, or bribe her, or any of the other underhanded things you had done in the past to control me. You lose." Abby smiled at her husband looking like a cat that had caught a mouse, and he turned towards her, sputtering.

Okay, I admit it. I was lost.

I was also significantly concerned that she was using those reasons as her evaluation process for her trainers. Talent should be higher than a trainer's ability to not take bullying from someone else. Then again, that was *a kind of* moral. And morals should be higher than talent. Abby may be right.

Also, go me.

Abby's husband turned even redder, but my threat to call the cops seemed to have been effective as he turned and walked out the door without another word.

I turned to Abby. "Did you just slow clap me?" Okay. That was supposed to be 'I'm so sorry for your loss', but I guessed we could start with the slow clap.

In turn, Abby shot me a slight smile and shrugged.

"He's a bully who thinks he can always get his way because we have too much money. I enjoy watching him get put in his place."

Well, alrighty then. Score one for unprofessionalism.

"Can you stop him from bad-mouthing me? I mean, it isn't like I have a business that would be really hurt by it, but I'm trying to." I winced at the truth in my words and she gave me a slight smile.

"I can't stop him, but no one listens to him anyway. Forget it happened." She sat down in the other chair and braced herself. "Ok. I'm ready. Tell me what happened."

I went through the whole story. From when I got the call, to walking him and thinking he would be fine, to the decision to bring him in anyway.

"I don't know what happened, Abby. I really thought that bringing him in was a precaution. I thought he was over the worst of it. I'll never forget opening those doors and seeing him." My voice broke, and I dropped deeper into the chair. "I'm so sorry."

"I don't know what to say," Abby admitted.

I knew what she meant. When things like this happened, I always felt obligated to negate the other person's guilt, but she was the one that had lost an animal.

"I know you did your best," she continued, nodding to me, before her gaze went unfocused on the wall.

"My best wasn't good enough." It came out before I could stop it, and I winced again.

"No, it wasn't." Abby quietly agreed, but her tone held no malice. "Connor is getting him scheduled for a necropsy?"

"He said he would do it himself. He was feeling guilty about not noticing how bad the situation was either. He promised he would find out what we missed."

She nodded and looked away, staring back at the wall for a second. "What do I do now? Is there something for me to sign? Or pay for? I need to do something." She got up and started pacing.

"I can get the office person to give you the paperwork to sign, if you would like. I can also stay with you." She looked so lost and my heart broke a little more.

She might not have had a strong connection with Bon, but she had loved him in her own way.

"No. Just get me someone to give me the paperwork. I would prefer to grieve at home."

With Mr. Happy? If he were my husband, I would've rather stayed here, but she seemed to handle him, so I didn't want to judge. I just found the office girl and set Abby up with getting all the details closed out. While I watched her, another vet, Dr. Miller, came over.

"Lark, we've got your trailer clear. You can leave now."

I nodded and grabbed my keys.

"Abby, you sure you don't want me to stay?" Please say no, I silently begged. I needed a long cry and a warm bath.

"No. There's nothing for you to do. Go home. You have a long drive and it's late. I'll contact you in the morning for his stuff."

I started walking to the door before I stopped and turned back.

"I'm so sorry, Abby. So, so sorry." I looked over at her, hoping that she could read my remorse on my face.

She only nodded, so I left.

Home had never felt so far away, as it did right now.

CHAPTER 5

It was a little after midnight when I got home from the hospital.

I decided not to bother Gran and Hailey, preferring to grieve alone. Instead, I went to my house, climbing into my bed to cry all my frustrations into my pillow.

I hated failing.

It was even worse that I couldn't understand what I had missed. The voice in my head tried to remind me that sometimes these things happened, but I had never lost a horse so suddenly. In such a weird way.

At some point my crying must have turned into sleep, because my phone woke me up. Groggy, I blinked my way to the nightstand. With only one eye focusing on the phone screen, I tried to make the words flashing across my screen make sense.

Christy? Did that say Christy sent me a text? As in my best friend, and past student from when I lived back in San Francisco with Blake?

Christy: *What happened last night?*

Oh no. I was suddenly wide awake and scrambling to get the phone unlocked and read the other messages.

Blake: *Lark? What happened? Abby's husband is texting everyone that you killed his horse.*

Christy: *Abby's husband is blowing up everyone's phone.*

Shiitake balls. I guess he was going to make me put my money where my mouth was. I decided to text Christy back first.

Me: *What's he saying?*

Christy: *There you are! It's nine o'clock! I have been texting since eight.*

Me: *What's the…*

No. Calm down. I needed to not put anything in writing that could be used against me. Even to Christy.

Delete.

Me: *What's he saying?*

Christy: *That you ignored the signs of colic until the horse died and then drove the dead horse to the hospital, claiming it was alive when you put it in the trailer.*

That dung mucker, animal cookies.

Me: *It's a lie. The horse showed some signs of colic, but he was doing better when we put him in the trailer. He died en route. Is Abby or her vet saying anything?*

Christy: *Abby's friend, Janet, was here when my trainer told me about it. Janet said it was a lie, and that Abby said you did everything you could, but her husband is putting effort into telling as many people his lie as possible. If I were you, I would talk to a lawyer.*

Dung-tastic. I didn't want to spend money on a lawyer. And now I needed to call my absentee clients.

Emily: *You killed him. You should've given him back to me and he would still be alive.*

Well, fabulous. Trust Emily to kick me when I was down. I let myself stick my tongue out at the screen but forced my attention back to the important things: my customers. A half hour and three cups of coffee later, I finished talking with my two absentee clients and reassured them that it was all lies, and I would be pressing a lawsuit as soon as I talked to a lawyer. All from my bed, because I may have been in panic mode, but was going to be comfortable while doing it.

I dropped my phone in disgust. I didn't want to talk to a lawyer. I liked my lawyer-free life like it was yesterday. Before everything went sideways.

Slipping out of bed, I texted Blake the story, and asked if he could spread it around for me, as well as a few other friends I knew in the business. It didn't look like Abby's husband's lies had taken much hold, but it also could be mostly because no one trusted anyone who called up people at seven in the morning to badmouth someone else. Evidently bothering people that early earned enemies. Good to know. Also, I really should find out what the man's name is. Since I might have to sue him.

Son of a biscuit.

Tired and depressed, I decided to do what I always did when unhappy. Go to the barn. When I got home last night, I had decided that today would be a sick day, since I was sleep-deprived and ahead of schedule now that Bon was gone, but that didn't mean I couldn't go in and spend time with them.

The horses had already been fed this morning, and Missy wasn't scheduled to come in, so it was only me. I turned out my personal horses, watching Bob and Twice buck and play with each other. My other horse, Greg, who was my primary show horse, wandered the arena looking for food he wasn't going to find in between coming back to make sure I was okay.

After two trips around the arena, Greg settled next to me, resting his head on my shoulder as I scratched under his chin. My shoulder was killing me, but after last night I was taking affection of any kind. His soft breath in my ear, and sweet nuzzles, reminded me that no matter the price at the end of the day, the short time I had with each of my animals was worth it. Luckily his fur was a good absorbent for my tears, and his snuggles bolstered my soul.

Once my spirits had lifted from watching them play, I took on the barn. I was too upset to jump on a horse, so I decided to clean out Bon's stall and get all his stuff ready for transport. I knew Billy would clean it when he came back later tonight to clean and feed, but I couldn't let it sit there, mocking me.

Grabbing a pitchfork and a wheelbarrow, I swung the door open and started stripping the stall as I thought of all the reasons a horse might die suddenly like that. When I was on my third rendition of the evils of colic, I decided to try to think of anything but Bon.

Anything else but the colic. And my failure.

Or Brecken.

Anything at all.

Nope.

The only thing my brain gave me was Brecken.

Great. Well, if nothing else, it wasn't thinking about the horse. Or my failure. Yep. We were definitely not going down that rabbit hole again.

"Lark?"

Wow. I thought of him and he appeared.

"Brecken?" I poked my head out of the stall to look down the aisle. He stood at the end of the barn, hesitating as he tried to locate me. When he saw me, his shoulders relaxed slightly, and he walked toward me, stopping when he reached the stall door.

I was struggling with seeing him again, as part of my getting-over-the-possibility-of-Brecken plan had been convincing myself that no one was *that* attractive. Then he showed up and reminded me. Maybe I should run my hands through his hair so that I knew it wasn't soft and silky like my mind thought it would be.

"I didn't come back for you." His response came out quick, with barely any spaces between the words.

"Okay?" I didn't know how to respond. 'Good' and 'how dare you not come back for me' were neck and neck, and I could see the crazy in both responses.

"I mean, I want to take you out while I'm here, but I don't want to pressure you into thinking I was here just for you." He reached up with one of his hands to rub the back of his neck, and I got lost in his biceps for a second before refocusing.

Well, okay then. I was not sure where to go with that. That was what I wanted. Maybe? I didn't know. I still felt pretty rejected.

"I think I'm good with what you're saying, but there's a part of me that feels like I should be offended," I answered honestly.

"Okay... can we stick with the first part of your emotions?"

I didn't know.

I tried to think about it, but I was out of the energy needed to feel strongly about... well... anything.

"Sure." Anything to get out of this conversation. "You aren't here for me, but you would like to go on a date. Oh, wait. You didn't say date. Did you mean a date?"

His eyes widened for a moment before he grinned slightly.

"I think this has to hold the record for the most awkward date invitation ever," he confessed. "But I'm glad you interpreted my social bumbling correctly."

Now he had me laughing.

"For me personally?" I pointed at myself as I leaned on the pitchfork. "Nope. My ex invited me to go to a show with him, as a groom, so I could see what an Eventing show was like. You know, the shows where they jump over the obstacles out on a trail? It wasn't until we were there that I found out he told everyone we were dating."

His mouth dropped at Blake's audacity. "You had gone out before, though, right?"

I chuckled at my stupid younger self.

"Nope. That was the first time we were alone without friends. God, I was stupid. That should have been my first clue."

"How young were you?" He leaned on the stall, relaxing as he enjoyed my ex's stupidity.

"Nineteen? Maybe. Too young. But I had a good barn going, and he got so many people interested when he was with me. To be fair, I got my fair share of people from his name being attached to mine. I just shouldn't have confused love with success. How about you? Is this the most awkward date invite you have ever had? Or given, I guess."

That got me a full smile, and even though it wasn't as dazzling as Connor's, it had an honest warmth that made me uncomfortably happy to be the cause of it. Connor's smiles were freely given. Brecken's had to be earned.

"By far. I haven't had a lot of time to date, and when I did it was more of just accepting the offers given. They chased me down, hoping they could make me change my bachelor ways, I guess." We both winced, me at the girls' stupidity and him at what it said about him.

"Oh please. Your bachelor ways? Or your workaholic ways?"

He grinned at me and nodded, admitting I was right.

"So, you have never asked a girl out?" I demanded, curious.

"Yes, I have." He thought about the answer for a minute. "Just not recently."

"How not recent?"

"Not in the past ten years?" He winced, and I laughed.

"You need to be kidding. You haven't asked a girl out in *ten* years?" Okay, I was feeling special now.

"Nope. I don't date much. Work doesn't leave me time." He shrugged as if he was fine with it, then looked down at the ground.

"Wow. You should do something about that." Hint, hint.

"Yeah, I've been thinking that recently, too. Want to help me make a decision?" His gaze swung up, his eyes grabbing mine and his lips curling up into a slight smirk.

"That sounds like a lot of pressure. What decision?" Because I was hoping we were still on the dating thing. Was he not? Hopefully it wasn't whether he should stay here or not. That's a no-win answer for me.

"Is asking a girl out better than being asked out?" He stood up and moved closer to the stall and me.

I laughed, relaxing now that the pressure felt gone.

"So, this date would be like a 'test date'?" I couldn't help moving a little closer to him. Maybe I could get that answer for Jen. It wasn't like him being closed off for two weeks was that big a deal. I was making too much out of it…

"Would that get you to say 'yes'?"

"No. But if you stopped beating around the bush, I might say 'yes' to a straight up invitation." *Please ask... please ask...*

"Will you go to dinner with me tonight?" His lips were now in a full smirk. He thought he had me.

"Did you already talk to my grandmother?"

He blushed.

Okay, less sexy, but I was still interested. "Sure, but not dinner. Maybe drinks. I want to see Hailey tonight since I didn't get to see her last night."

He nodded and smiled while I went back to cleaning the stall to hide my exhilaration.

"Mind if I stick around here for a while?" he asked. The butterflies in my stomach that were making fluttery sensations sped up. He wanted to keep talking to me.

"I guess that's fine." I dumped some shavings and went back for more. "So why do you talk to my grandmother more than you talk to m—" My words cut off when I saw something green sitting at the top of the wheelbarrow where I had dumped my last load. Was that a flower? Wait, I think I knew that flower. But why was it in Bon's stall? I looked to check his windows, which were still closed to fight off the night chill. I reached over to grab it, squinting at it harder, trying to tell myself I was jumping to conclusions.

"Lark? Is something wrong?"

"Do you have a camera?" My phone was in the tack room.

"On my phone. Why?" I handed him the flower and looked around the stall for others. I found two more in the corner beneath the feeder.

"Come take a picture of this, will you?"

"Sure." He walked in and took a picture of the flowers sitting in the stall. "You want to tell me why?"

"Because I'm pretty sure that those flowers are Oleander."

"As in the poison?"

"The poison. It's frequently used in government landscaping all over the state because it's pretty and easy to upkeep. We learned how to recognize the plant on sight, and I'm pretty sure that those are the leaves. Can you Google to confirm?"

He nodded and pulled up the Oleander flower.

Yep.

Yay me for remembering. Bad because I was right.

Bon didn't die from colic.

CHAPTER 6

"What do I do now?" I asked Brecken. "I mean, do I report this to the cops? Or does someone else deal with animal crimes?" I watched as his gaze went blank and he turned away from me to stare at my training board.

"Not to be insensitive, but how much was Bon Voyage worth?" he asked, still not looking back at me.

"He was insured at eight hundred thousand dollars," I answered off the top of my head, then swallowed hard. Did he think...? No. But... I moved until I could look Brecken in the eye. "You think he was killed for the insurance money?" Horses worth the kind of money that Bon had been, were generally insured for death and health issues.

"Can you think of another reason?"

Well, yeah. Maybe. But I didn't want to say that to a police officer. Unfortunately, looking away instead of answering the question kind of, well, answered the question.

"Lark. Who else would have an interest in poisoning the horse?" He moved so I had to put effort into not looking at him.

Too bad for him, I was willing to put in the effort. I stared at the flowers, biting the side of my lip, debating if I should tell him. I mean, she probably had an alibi, right? I should tell him everything.

"The old trainer. Emily Reed was very upset about the horse moving. I guess Abby didn't tell her and she found out when the horse was being trailered out here. She showed up at the barn that day, screaming at me about how I stole her horse."

"She was angry?"

"Very. She felt Bon was the horse that was going to take her to the Olympics. He was the best horse in her barn. Losing him was a huge hit." I risked glancing up at him.

"And to yours?" His face was shuttered, and I couldn't tell what he was thinking. That bothered me a little, but I tried not to show it.

"I guess. I mean, had I showed him and was able to reverse his slump, then he would have been huge. Losing him like this, without being able to show him? The only real loss to my barn is the damage Abby's husband is trying to do to my reputation."

"Abby's husband is coming after you, personally?" He sounded angry, so I risked another glance.

Yep. He looked angry. The butterflies in my stomach that took flight at that thought, were probably inappropriate.

"Yes. He's saying that I ignored the signs of colic until the horse was dead, and then transported it to the hospital, claiming that it died en route to cover up for my lax caretaking. My clients want me to sue, but my lawyer said it's going to be almost impossible to prove damages." I was rambling as he wrote that down in his notebook.

I frowned. I didn't remember him getting the notebook out. That meant he went from Brecken, the potential romantic interest, to Brecken, the cop. Now that I thought about it, he switched when his face went blank. I saw it, but for some reason didn't really see it for what it was. Stupid me. Well, I might as well be useful. "Do you need Abby's last name?"

"Harris. Abigail and Tony Harris," he supplied, then looked up at me with a grimace.

Yep. I was on to him now. Disappointment shot through me.

"Well, at least you told me the truth. You are not here for me. At all." I was unimpressed with his sigh, too angry to do anything but continue to stare a hole in him.

"No. I didn't come back here for you, although I can't say that you didn't factor into taking the assignment." He tucked the notebook away and crossed his arms, as I watched him through narrowed eyes. "I still would like to go on that date. It wasn't related. I swear."

"So, you aren't on vacation." That would also explain the 'bad idea' comment. He had been right. It had been a bad idea.

"No. That was my cover to work in the area without people knowing. We were trying to keep this quiet."

"Why?" As soon as the word left my lips the answer came to me. "Because of Bon? That's why you made contact after so long? Why you are here this morning? Who are you investigating? Abby or her husband?"

Brecken's face went so hard I bet I could've cracked granite on it. Which was good, because I really wanted to throw some things at it. Or cry. Donkey bits. I refused to cry in front of him.

"I can't tell you anything about my investigation." His cheek twitched.

"Nope." Of course he wouldn't. "Because why would you tell me? So I could've protected my charge?" I scoffed. "Let me guess... I didn't need to know that there was a risk?" I turned away from him, trying to keep my emotions in check. "You know what? Get out."

"Lark, I only got here yesterday. And honestly, I don't know that there's any connection to the horse. It looks like it was a coincidence that we were here investigating, and you got Tony's horse."

He was just trying to make me cooperate, so I crossed my arms and stared.

He frowned at my response before his face went blank again. He was done trying to explain himself to me. "Could those leaves have blown in?" He asked, still in police mode.

I felt that I was obligated, since Bon had been in my care, to answer Brecken's question, but I scowled the whole time.

"No. There are no large sources of Oleander in the surrounding areas and none on property. The only place locally that you can find it would be in a private garden. That was something I always look at when I move into a new barn. So no, several flowers would not be able to just happen to congregate in one stall." I gripped my arms, digging my nails in as I answered, trying to be helpful and short at the same time.

"How much does a horse need to consume for it to be deadly?"

"Very little. But they don't like the taste, so most horses don't eat it, even when available. Bon must have eaten one and then not touched the rest."

"And that's common? Most horse people would know that horses don't like the taste?"

"I would think so? Or maybe only the ones that live where Oleander is planted. I don't really know how popular that knowledge is outside of the local barns. The city where I used to ride used it as landscaping, so we all were told to keep an eye out for it. I'm kind of surprised I could recognize it after a few years."

"And you know of no local source?" That sounded suspiciously like an accusation.

"No. I would have no idea where to get it." That was all the information I felt like sharing right now. "Now get out. I have stalls to strip, just in case there are more flowers." And a bruised heart to mend. Again. I pushed past him, picking up the wheelbarrow and pushing it towards the ramp to dump it. He followed, trailing behind me as we left the barn, heading towards the back of the parking lot where the ramp was.

"Lark?"

No. I didn't want to play nice anymore. Could we not?

"What?"

He could hear my teeth snap together at the end of the word. He had no illusions that I was pissed.

"That might be evidence. I need you to not take that away." His voice was soft, and it took me a moment to process what he said.

Another sarcastic laugh escaped me.

"It's amazing that a few days ago, I thought getting body parts delivered to my door was the worst thing that had ever happened to me. Tell me, Brecken, why is it that everything bad in my life seems to have you directly attached?" I dropped the wheelbarrow where it was at the end of the parking lot and turned to him, hoping that if I glared hard enough, the tears might not come. This was my business. The one place I was really good. Where I had all the answers. And now some man, who didn't know what he was talking about, was trying to ruin my reputation, and police were investigating my barn for a possible poisoning. I would be lucky to have a client by the end of the night.

"We need to search the stables."

Yeah. Saw that coming.

"Can I put the rest of the horses into turnouts so you can search their stalls?"

He nodded, and I went to move them. Luckily, I had just enough turnouts to let everyone have their own space, except my three, who were still in the jumping arena. I made sure that everyone had water and could stay until tomorrow morning or whenever the police released my barn. So long as no one tried to pet Twice, everyone would be fine. They all knew her reputation by now. The horses should be fine.

Brecken supervised the whole time, alternating between his professional police persona and glances that made me think he was regretting how our conversation ended. But I didn't give him an inch. I was too mad to talk to him right now, and I wasn't ready to admit that I really didn't have much of a leg to stand on. He had told me he wasn't there for me. He hadn't made any promises. He only obliquely asked me out. I should not be hurt to learn the only reason he was back was for work. I knew he was a workaholic. I needed to stop hoping it would change.

Oh, god. I stopped dead in my tracks, pretending that I was studying the horses in the turnouts.

I was like all the other women, hoping he would change for me. I couldn't believe I was still this dumb. There should be a rule: once a woman turned thirty, she should get an automatic upgrade that stopped stupid things like trying to change people and falling for romantic lies. Especially the lies we tell ourselves. But since no such upgrade existed, I was going to have to muddle through, trying to contain my emotions in the bounds of logic.

Because that always worked.

Maybe if he was a little less handsome. Or nice. Or funny. Or hadn't rescued that pit bull from the bay last year.

Maybe I should go ram my head against a wall until it started picking better men.

I walked back towards the barn as techs were starting to arrive. John, our town detective, and another man, dressed in a suit and tie, walked up to me and I stopped to assess the newest man, trying to figure out where he fit in.

"Lark." John knew I was pissed, and his greeting lacked warmth and eye contact.

That's right. I was not happy to be pulled into this bull pucky. Whatever it was. I was less happy that he knew that Brecken was coming, and why Brecken was here and had never told me. What if knowing that his owner was a criminal could have let me save Bon?

"John."

"Sorry we had to come out here," he said to the ground. Brecken came up behind him, also not meeting my eyes, so I turned to the newest addition to our little gathering. He hadn't gotten the memo, I guessed, since he had no issue meeting my eyes.

"Who are you?" I demanded, crossing my arms over my chest.

"Unimportant." He barely gave me a glance before scanning the grounds. He then studied the barn, ignoring me completely.

What was up with this? Did he think he was a secret spy or something? Or a Jedi? All he needed was to wave his hand in front of my face, telling me that he was not the cop I was looking for, and hope I was going to ignore his presence? Yeah. That was not happening.

"So, is Unimportant your first name or your last? Or is it your job title?"

Well, that got me eye contact from all three of the men. John's eyebrows were reaching for his hairline and I could see the corners of his mouth creeping up as he tried to hide a smile. Brecken's eyes were just as wide, but he was too afraid to draw more attention to himself.

Good idea, buddy.

Mr. Unimportant focused on me, eyes narrow and aggressively steady as he tried to dominate me into submission.

That only worked when I was not pissed. Try again later.

"It means that it isn't relevant information for you to know."

He did not…. Wrong day.

"Your name? You really think that your NAME is that important? Or that the whole town doesn't know who you are already?"

"*You* don't know it, so that isn't an unfounded assumption." One eyebrow crept up as he challenged me. "And I said my name is *un*-important. As in I *don't* think it's 'that important'."

The snark was strong with this one. He did spare me enough attention to throw me a smirk, but I just smiled. Ok. It might have been an evil smile, but it showed my teeth and my mouth had upturned corners, so it counted. I was starting to love these city boys. There was something they never took into account. I caught John's wince, so I knew that they had already been to the police office. That meant…. I checked my phone. Ahh. There it was.

"FBI Special Agent Nicholas Kelly. Huh. Here for an insider trading investigative task force… Interesting."

"What the…" Special Agent Kelly grabbed the phone from my hand and started reading.

I couldn't help my smile from spreading. It was fun to watch other people get Lindsey'ed. John lost his fight, and covered his smile with his hand, which was good since he was the next one the FBI agent turned to.

"How did this happen?" Special Agent Kelly demanded, thrusting the phone into John's face.

John put his hands up, exposing his grin but still trying to look innocent.

"Remember when I told you we should meet with the Chief at the diner?" John asked as he shook his head and a chuckle escaped. "And *you* insisted it wasn't professional? That, there, is the reason."

By this time, Brecken had taken the phone and was reading.

"Well, at least she didn't mention me in this. Just the two of you. I'm still here chasing Lark, so she doesn't know I'm a part of the task force."

Well, there went my amusement. My frown came back as I remembered I was his cover.

"Um… about that. Lark…" John started, but my angry glance stopped him.

Hah! Now they wanted me to cover for them. Nope.

"I'm telling Jen. Over drinks. That Brecken will be paying for. I *might* be convinced not to tell the sewing circle if…" John and Brecken were both hanging on my words. Special Agent Kelly wasn't, but who cared. What do I want? "… Brecken goes home."

They both winced. Not good.

"I don't know if that's possible," John admitted. "Brecken is the contact person for the San Francisco PD. It's a joint task force, with the FBI, SFPD and us, all working Tony's case."

I was relieved. Wait. I wasn't supposed to be relieved. I just asked for them to make him go home. Why would I be happy when he had to stay?

Brecken, who was still staring at my phone, suddenly turned white, locked it and jerked it behind him. Yeah, that isn't obvious or anything.

"Brecken. Give me my phone."

"Nope."

"Brecken!"

"Trust me, you don't want to see it."

Fudge buckets.

"I'm going home. Keep the blooming phone."

"What does 'blooming' mean? Is this a nowhere-California thing?" Special Agent Kelly asked John as I walked away.

For the love of…

CHAPTER 7

G oing home early as the cops searched my barn for any evidence of foul play, I decided to stop by Gran's house. Brecken had given me my phone back before I left, but I was avoiding Lindsey's blog and whatever it was that was going to upset me.

Gran would make it all better.

Right after she told me.

Please let there be cookies. Or alcohol. Or both.

Yeah, please let there be both.

I debated where she might be at this time of day. Sometimes Gran still slipped into the Tea House to work a shift when my aunt wasn't looking, but I had a feeling she would be home today. Or maybe it was just a hope. Either way, it was for naught when I got a call right as I was about to pull in.

"Jen?" I was surprised to hear from her today.

"Hey, Lark. What's up?"

"Umm... isn't that my line since you called me?"

Silence. From this call, I was guessing her day had not improved since yesterday. Distraction needed stat. She needed me to be funny.

"Good point. So, I need information." Jen's voice pulled me back to the conversation.

Okay, I could work with that. Well, since there were no specifics on the information…

"It's physically impossible to lick your own elbow." I got silence again, but I was pretty sure the reason was different. Then I heard a clunk.

"Sorry…. Sorry! I dropped the phone."

"You just tried it." I couldn't help the snort of laughter.

"Of course I did. It could have been a joke. Plus, I do yoga. It's supposed to let me do all kinds of weird twisty things. Isn't that why we go?"

"I went because I needed better posture. You started going for better sex. I don't know why you still go."

"That was a brutal way of saying I'm not getting any."

"In the past few years, you've had more than I have." It came out bitter. Turned out I could still reach a point where I missed sex. I refused to admit how much the timing of my longings and Brecken's original arrival in town coincided. Even after these few weeks, I was still a little surprised at the change. After my ex, and finding out how close I was to multiple STDs, I thought I would never want sex again.

"That would console me, but you turned into a nun since your divorce. Which reminds me. How was Brecken this morning?"

I felt my eyebrows rise as I contemplated the phone.

"How did you know I saw him this morning?"

"Umm… he mentioned that he was going to go see you last night. After you left the bar."

I snorted into the phone. Yeah, that was believable. I was starting to put two and two together. Well, in this case I was putting 'insider trading' and stressed out CPA together, but whatever.

"I'm guessing he mentioned it when he talked to you about how he was there to investigate the insider trading case on my clients?"

"Shit. They told you?" She hesitated. "Wait, Tony Harris was your client?"

"Well, his wife was. Brecken accidentally admitted knowing my client's names when I found the poison in Bon's stall—"

"Wait! Back that up. You found poison in the horse's stall? The one that died?"

"Yes." I couldn't get more out around the lump in my throat.

"I'm sorry. When did you find out about the poison?"

"I found it this morning when I was cleaning his stall and talking to Brecken."

"Have you let the vet know?"

Good point. Mental note to do that as soon as I was done here.

"No, and thank you for that reminder. Anyway, he was there beating around the date bush and letting me know that he wasn't here chasing me—"

"Which you wouldn't want," Jen reminded me.

I scowled at the phone and wished for a glare button. This phone had everything else. Why not a glare button?

I knew I didn't want him to do some big romantic gesture. I acknowledged that I told everyone I wanted slow and cautious. But being told he wasn't chasing, wasn't fun either.

Wait! Text message. I got this. Angry face emoji sent, and my point made, I continued.

"Which would be weird," I agreed, "and the nerves seemed cute. Until I found out that he was there investigating someone and using 'not chasing me' as a cover. Then he just happened to know my client's names before I could tell him. And then he called in John who had Mr. 'Unimportant' with him—"

"What? Who is Mr. 'Unimportant'?"

"Nicholas—"

"Kelly." She let out a long sigh. "Ass hat."

Okay. I pulled my truck lever back into drive. This conversation needed to be had in person. "I'm coming over."

"No, it's—"

"Don't bother. I'm coming over. My business may be in ruins and I might not have any clients at all tomorrow. You owe me knowing about Mr...." Ok. I was stuck here. I was partial to Mr. Unimportant because I had the history, but Mr. Ass Hat was a classic. I took too long deciding.

"You can't decide what to call him now, can you?" Jen's voice clearly carried her amusement to me.

"Yeah, it's a problem. I really like Mr. Unimportant, because, well, it's amazing, but Mr. Ass Hat has just got that vibe, you know?"

"It's a tough call." She was clearly humoring me, but I was ready to make this into a thing. "Also, you amuse yourself too much."

"Yes, yes I do. But, no, really. Maybe I should call up Lindsey. She could do a poll on her blog. We could get the whole town in on this."

"OK, rein it in, girl. We're not getting the whole town involved in a nickname for a man who will be gone tomorrow."

"You sure?"

"Yes! We don't need the whole—"

"No! Not that. That he'll be gone tomorrow."

"Yes. Absolutely. Leaving. No reason to stay. Taking a hike. Riding off into the sunset. Gone like Donkey Kong."

"Yeah, you had me until the last one. He's going to be staying a while?"

"Until they find what they are looking for." The bitter note in her voice told me she was frustrated and stressed.

"And you don't know where that is?"

"No clue. If I had I would have thrown it at Ass Hat's head this morning."

"Mr. Unimportant." I corrected.

"Lark."

"Yes?"

"I hate you."

"I'm hanging up. My job here is done. See you in a few minutes." I laughed as I hung up. Poor Jen. She makes my life complete.

I dialed Connor, expecting to get his voice mail.

"Hello?"

Huh. I have never had a vet answer their phone this much. I usually left messages or talked to their phone service. It was nice to be able to get a hold of him so easily, but it was also... really freaking weird. Made me wonder if he was struggling. No. That wasn't nice. He probably gave me his personal line. Abby was an important client. Maybe this was what VIP treatment felt like.

"Hey, Connor. It's Lark."

"Hey, Lark! How are you doing? What can I do for you?"

"I was wondering if you tested Bon for Oleander poisoning."

The other side of the call went quiet before his voice came back on the line, his tone clearly puzzled. "I can. Should I?"

"I found leaves in his stall this morning, buried in the shavings."

"Wow! How are the other horses?"

"Good. So far they were only in Bon's stall."

"Damn. I never would have... Yeah. I'll rush the results."

"Thanks. Oh! And the cops might need a copy."

"Why?" There was silence from his side while he processed. "They couldn't be thinking insurance fraud? Abby doesn't seem like type."

"Yeah. I don't think so either. Plus, why pay to move him if you were just going to kill him within days?"

"So, they think it was the husband?"

Hah! I wasn't the only one who didn't like Abby's husband.

"Well, *I* think so. But you know the police. Don't like to tell people anything." At least, Brecken didn't. The rest of the Barrow Bay police department was a little more open-minded, as Lindsey continually reminded us through her articles.

"Yeah. I know what you mean."

Hmm. That sounded more serious than I had expected. Or at least personal. Had he had a run in with the police before?

"I should have those results to you tomorrow," he continued. "I thought I might deliver them to you personally. Maybe... maybe take you up on your offer to show me around town?"

Oh. Wow. I had pushed that out of my mind. With Bon's death and all the drama around it, I didn't know if right now was a good time to start dating. I was still trying to process my emotions. I failed. Did I really want to fail again? Maybe I should focus on the barn, and retaining my clients, and fixing my reputation, but... then again, maybe spending some time away from all that would be good for me. Plus, well, maybe he could help me put Brecken in perspective. Maybe if Brecken isn't the only fish in my sea, I might not be so... pathetic.

"Sure. Yes! It's a date." Oh no. Overstatement.

"Yep. It's a date. See you soon."

That might have been a horrible decision. Really bad. But...

Sigh.

I drove the block and a half to Jen's house, pulling up as she opened the door, hitting me with her best glower. Oops. I should probably tone it down a little the next time I was trying to distract her.

"Ass Hat and company are heading this way."

Ha! The look wasn't for me. *And Shiitake mushrooms.* I thought about what would happen if we stayed here. Nope.

"Run?" I offered. Really, we would be driving, but semantics seemed unimportant now.

"It's one in the afternoon. Where are we going to go?"

"The Pub?"

"Please. It's us. That's the first place Brecken and John will look."

"The coffee shop?" *Snickerdoodles.* That was closed still. Why did I even suggest that?

"I lied. That would have been the first. If it wasn't still closed. The Pub will be second. And please. We need to be less predictable."

"I don't see you throwing out any suggestions!" I lifted my eyebrows in a silent challenge.

"That's because there's only one place I can think of where they won't go, even if we're visible from the street." She smiled at me, but it wasn't her happy smile. More like her...

No. She couldn't mean... *fudge buckets*. Not there. "No. No! I refuse!"

"Oh, come on. It's not the bowels of hell."

"Yes, it is!" I grabbed her doorway and prepared to hold on. She just watched, shaking her head.

"Don't you think you're being slightly dramatic?"

"No! I'm not being dramatic."

"You ran into a barn one month ago to save your saddles from a killer with a gun. This isn't nearly as bad."

"One, I didn't know about the gun. Two, saddles AND my horses. Both. They are my babies—"

"I wish you were just talking about the horses, but I know you mean the horses and the saddles," Jen muttered.

"Five thousand dollars a saddle, Jen! Five thousand. At least. And no resale value. Insurance doesn't cover that kind of replacement cost!"

"It's a saddle. Get cheaper ones."

I glared but gave up on making her understand and moved on. "THREE —"

"Oh, here we go again."

"THREE, they'll make me talk about feelings. FEELINGS, Jen."

"Oh, the horror! Talking about your emotions like a normal, well-adjusted person! Oh no!"

I scowled. It didn't seem to affect her as she melodramatically flung her hand to her forehead, swooned around the room, mocking the old Victorian age movies while never actually landing anywhere before she moved again to swoon somewhere else. Okay. That was funny. And I guess I was being a little over the top.

"Fine," I grumbled. "Let's go process my emotions." I still wasn't going to be enthusiastic about it, though.

"Good." She rubbed her hands together with a smile. "I need more tea anyway."

I figured I got played. "Truck or your car?"

"Truck. It looks better if you kidnapped me."

"I don't like the sound of that." I didn't know if I could afford to be her accomplice right now.

"Nope, but Gladys texted me over social media so there's no record of her warning. We're in the clear."

I didn't know what was more disturbing. The fact that it was starting to sound like we were running from the cops or that Gladys knew how to send an untraceable message through social media. Why were all the old woman in this town cooler than me?

I drove us to the tea shop, which was the first building on Main Street. Well, on the ocean side. It was a two-story, old-fashioned cottage, with the tea shop in front and judgment in the back in the form of my family, who all helped my grandmother run the place. The whole top floor, as well as the back porch and the back rooms were dedicated to the High Tea service, which was usually full. During the summer months reservations were required, but since the season had ended, the high tea should have a table or two open. Oh joy.

Gran had worked out a deal with Olivia, our local baker, years ago to bring in the cookies and desserts, which had made the tea a hit years ago. Also helped promote Olivia's bakery after her husband died, so it was a win/win for both of them.

Since then, Gran added a chef named Pierre. To my delight, he said everything in a French accent and swore in French when stressed. Which was impressive considering he was from Kentucky. Dorothy had found him during a business trip and brought him home, like a lost puppy. From what Gran told me, they both showed up at the shop's door one morning. Pierre walked right past Gran saying that he needed room to make perfection, then poked his head out of the kitchen to add that he needed the tea list. If he was going to make food to accent them, he needed to know what teas we carried. It was love at first demand. How a French-trained chef from Kentucky became obsessed with tea, I didn't know. The whole town had been glad not to have to let Aunt Helen cook anymore.

Ding. I pulled my phone out to see a message from Gran.

Gran: *I'm picking up Hailey since it's a half day today. Picking her up at your normal time at my house? Or is your schedule off because of the cops this morning?*

Me: *Or you could meet us at the tea house right now.*

Me: *Wait. How did you know about the cops?*

Gran: *You are hiding in the Tea House? And, how do you think? Lindsey.*

Sigh. This was where I should have shame at our wussy actions and hide our purpose. I'm just going to be the bigger person and ignore Lindsey.

Me: *Yep. Want to join us?*

Gran: *Who's with you? Just you and Jen?*

Me: *Yep.*

Gran: *What happened with Brecken?*

Feelings. I could see the conversation about my feelings coming a mile away. But why not invite everyone to the same place at the same time. Aunt Helen would just tell her everything anyway. At least this way I would get to see Hailey.

Me: *Guess you are going to have to come here to find out.*

Gran: *See you in twenty.*

"Gran and Hailey are coming to meet us." I told Jen as I looked up from my phone.

"Good." Jen rubbed her hands together. "There's no way the boys are stupid enough to bother us in the Tea Shop when she's there."

I was enabling a monster.

"So, am I in the loop enough to know what's happening?" It would have to wait, since as we walked in the door, my aunt Helen saw us coming in and rushed over. As I watched her approach, I very seriously debated running for real.

"Lark! Jen! What a surprise. Goodness. Tea for three?"

Three? That isn't promising. Who was the third? Was she planning to sit with us?

"Four. Gran and Hailey will be here soon."

"So, five then. Good. Good. Right this way."

Five? Jen mouthed at me.

Your fault. This is your fault, I mouthed back. She looked confused, but the alarm was starting to win out.

"I'm so glad you decided to come in today. I didn't want to wait until the Sewing Circle tonight to get the gossip."

Oh, no. Maybe I could still make a run for it... My aunt grabbed my arm. Nope. Stuck. Why did I let Jen talk me into this? I sent her a long look, but she was too busy watching my aunt, her forehead furrowing in concern.

"What gossip?" I asked. I needed to strike first to find out what she knew. Life lessons I had learned from growing up in this family.

"Brecken. The vet. Who will you choose?"

We had reached the table and my aunt pulled me down into a chair, while she slid into another. Suddenly Gladys was in the third seat, Dorothy hot on her tail to slide into the fourth. Jen glanced around to make sure no one else was going to appear before she sat down. I was now staring down four gazes, all focused on getting an answer.

"Um, do I have to choose?"

"Why, Lark." Gladys fanned herself slightly while leaning forward as if to whisper something to me, but she missed her own memo because she used her full voice when she spoke. "Is this one of those threesome things we hear about? Like in those books?"

Threesome?

Books?

Oh lord. I didn't know where to start. Oh, wait.

"No. No! NO!" I looked around, sure that I would find Lindsey hiding behind a plant, waiting to tell everyone I wanted a threesome. "Why would you think I wanted…? No!" I scowled at all of them, giving Jen an extra-long one. She was enjoying this.

"Well, then, sweetheart, you're going to have to pick one." Gladys patted the back of my hand soothingly.

It was a commentary about my day that I needed the pats she was giving me. I *was* in need of a little soothing.

"Since I haven't gone out with either, I'm going to save any decision-making until after the date."

"So, there are dates?" my aunt interrupted.

"No! Yes. Well, Connor has a date. Brecken has a…" Jen kicked me under the table, shooting me a glare. Oh. Yeah. They didn't want me to tell the gossip queens about the case. Fine.

"A case?" Dorothy supplied. Jen and I both looked at her in surprise and Gladys winced. Dorothy waved away all our reactions. "Please. I got the call three days ago from some of my friends. The FBI putting a freeze on Abby's accounts got around within the hour it happened." Dorothy had more contacts in the business world than anyone I knew, and my father had been a stock broker. A very good one. She probably knew the minute the SEC was on the case.

"Wait? Their accounts are frozen?" How was she going to pay me? *Shiitake mushrooms. Not the point right now.*

"Just her husband's and their joint accounts. Abby's private accounts are fine."

Whew.

"When did that happen?" I asked Dorothy.

She glanced at Jen, who looked down at her napkin.

"Maybe I should go check on the—" Jen started only to be cut off by Dorothy.

"Three days ago."

After I had gotten Bon in the barn. I felt a little sick.

"So? When are you going out with them?" Aunt Helen interrupted.

Really? A horse was dead, as was my career, and they really wanted to talk about my love life? I looked around. They really did.

"Connor and I have a date tomorrow. When he brings me the results from the necropsy. Brecken..." I didn't know. I hadn't cancelled our date, but I felt it was pretty clear that I was feeling betrayed. If you got a date under false pretenses it was understood that it was cancelled when the other person figured it out. Right?

"Brecken?" My aunt prompted. "When's your date with him?"

"Didn't Dorothy just tell you? He's here for a case."
Now I was the one trying to find a waiter. Waitress.
Busboy. Anyone to postpone their answer.

"Oh please. An excuse," Dorothy dismissed.

"The truth. I'm not fooling myself again. Nor am I
falling for another man who uses me to further his own
career."

Oh. OH.

Well, that was unintentionally revealing. But it
stopped everyone. Well, it stopped Jen and my aunt,
who looked away uncomfortably.

They knew my past. They knew my ex-husband.
How he used my talents to gain clients, my contacts to
spread his name. I had been an asset to him, although he
did admit I was an attractive asset. He even told me that
after I caught him cheating. Told me he was actually
attracted to me, like that would reduce the damage, but
he would have never married me if not for my riding
talent. How I had missed that tidbit during our eight-
year relationship? I kicked myself over it regularly. I
could tell that Dorothy guessed the truth from the way
her gaze dropped to the table, no longer meeting my
eyes. Only Gladys looked confused, glancing from each
person to the next, trying to figure out the part of the
story I hadn't said out loud.

"You coming to the Sewing Circle tonight?"
Dorothy asked as she got up, meeting my gaze again.

I nodded. Might as well. Sitting at home tonight,
thinking about the date I was refusing to go on, wasn't a
good option.

"Can I come?" Jen asked. We all turned to her, our mouths gaping. "What? It sounds… fun."

Wow. She's going to the Sewing Circle to avoid Mr. Unimportant. He must have really gotten to her.

"Sure. We would love to have you, Jen," Dorothy said, her eyes narrowed on Jen, who was making a concerted effort to not meet them. "And Lark, don't make the same mistakes I did. Don't judge someone by someone else's actions. Sometimes people need an external push to take a risk and go after what they want. Don't punish both of you for his hesitation." With that, Dorothy swept out of the tea house, Gladys following. My aunt, sensing that Dorothy had dropped a bomb on me, murmured something about getting us a tea serving and left.

I stared at the table in front of me. Was I judging Brecken from the pain that Blake had left? Maybe. But… was that wrong? Didn't pain teach us not to make the same mistakes? Where did I draw the line between logical hesitation and blind instincts?

I looked at Jen, who was shuffling in her seat, but her glance told me she was going to ask. Desperate times. Negotiation seemed the best option.

"I won't ask you about Special Agent Ass Hat if you don't ask about Brecken."

She glanced at me, slipping her lip in between her teeth as she weighed my offer.

"Deal."

We both nodded and turned to the three-tiered serving tray my aunt put on the table, loaded with only desserts instead of the normal sandwiches. She also had Jen's favorite tea. Apology for being nosy accepted.

We were talking about ways to make Bon's death seem less, well, deadly, when we heard Gran's voice.

"And who do you think you are, young man?" Her voice was cold and short. Someone was in trouble.

"What do you want to bet that Agent Ass Hat didn't listen to John." Jen commented, craning her neck trying to get a better view. When that failed, she looked at me.

We shouldn't.

With a giggle, we both got up and crept closer to the wall so we could peek around it. There. Now we could see everything.

"Ma'am, we need to talk to—"

"We? Who's 'we'?" Gran interrupted, glancing around like she couldn't see John's car right outside. With both John and Brecken waiting inside, their faces turned to watch.

I flipped back around the corner, debating if they could see me. "Jen! Can they see us?"

"Who? Brecken? No," she told me absently. "Now hush. I'm listening."

"...John will be in soon. We don't mean to interrupt your facilities, we just need to talk to—"

"Have you been to a high tea before?" Gran asked, her eyes narrowed as her arm wrapped around Hailey. Agent Ass Hat looked around at the people gathered but didn't back down. Snark and a backbone. I was starting to wish I had met him before I met Brecken.

Wait. I was single. I could hit on him if I wanted.

I looked at the ridiculously hot man in John's front seat. The one who laughed at my family's crazy antics and rescued drowning pit bulls from the Bay. The one who smiled at my jokes and moved across the nation to help his sister.

I didn't want anyone else. *Dagnabit.*

"No, I can't say I ha—" Agent Ass Hat started to say.

"Then let me tell you about it."

Uh oh. Warning. Warning.

"I don't know that I need—"

"Everyone needs high tea. It brings people together. It teaches us to stop and enjoy life. It—"

"I apologize for interrupting you, but I need to talk with—"

Gasp! Did he just cut her off? The whole house was now watching.

"No. I don't care who you want to talk to. Do you have a warrant?"

"No, it isn't—"

"Then get out. Wait. Helen, give him a sample. Free of charge. Maybe a little chamomile will get your head out of your ass. If a woman is refusing to come out to talk to you, you don't barge in like a bull. I know it's confusing to the males of our species, with all these 'alpha males' you see in media and books, but a real woman wants a man to respect her opinions. Respect her wants. You might want to try that next time before bursting in, demanding that she cater to your whims.

Your schedule. Good for her for making you wait. Now leave."

Gran didn't wait for him to comply before turning and walking towards our table. Even though I knew she could see us, we both kept our heads craned around the corner watching Special Agent Ass Hat decide what he was going to do. Uncle Flynn was coming up behind him to encourage the right decision when the special agent's phone went off. He read it and then gave the room a curt nod before walking out. We waited until we saw the car with John, Brecken, and the special agent drive off.

"Well. He gave up faster than I thought." Jen looked disappointed, her shoulders drooping as she turned to lead the way back to the table. Gran and Hailey were almost to us, but I was too interested in Jen's reaction to do much more than wave.

"Didn't we want him to give up?" I asked, sitting back in my chair and studying her face while she studied the desserts.

"Yeah. Sure. Whatever." She grabbed a chocolate tart and put it on her plate before picking it apart with her fork.

Yep. Totally believed her.

"You like him," I hissed under my breath. I had three seconds to finish this conversation before Gran and Hailey got here, so I was really just going for her reaction. Which I got. Wide eyes swung up to mine, as she opened her mouth for whatever denial she had come up with. I smiled in victory before turning away from her to greet Gran and Hailey.

"Lark! Jen! What a surprise," Gran said as she sat down. Hailey ran around the table to give me a big hug. I wrapped my arms around her, letting our love reset my world, even if just for a second.

"Hey, Hailey Bailey. How was school?" I asked her, still holding on as she backed up a little, trying to look me in the face.

"Good. I don't have homework."

"That's good." I pulled her back for another hug before I turned to Gran, who was watching us with a smile. "How are you doing, Gran?"

"Good." She sat down in an open seat, pulling her napkin into her lap before primly adjusting herself so she had perfect posture. At home, she may be my Gran, but when she was in the Tea House, she was every inch a lady. I straightened up, self-conscious about my own posture, and I saw Jen follow suit. Hailey sat down with perfect posture from the start. Yep. I really needed to get her away from Gran more. "So, I'm assuming we're hiding from the man I stopped from coming in here?"

Jen's posture slumped back down, and she went back to mauling her tart.

"Yep. His name is—" I tried to answer for Jen, but Gran shook off my reply.

"Special Agent Nicholas Kelly," she tsked. "Such an Irish name. Wonder if he is. Always liked those Irish men. Good in bed."

Blink.

I didn't think I heard that right.

I glanced at Jen, who was staring at my grandmother in horror, then to Hailey, who had covered her mouth and started giggling. Yep. She had said it.

"Gran!!" I hissed, jerking my head at Hailey. Cover story. I need a cover story. "Um, Hailey… sometimes adults like to… eat!… they like to eat in bed. And we rate them. But not by nationality. Because that's prejudiced. And we like to include everyone." What had just come out of my mouth?

"How do you rate them by eating? Is there a guide to bed manners like Gran made me read about table manners?" Hailey asked, her innocent eyes looking up at me from under her eyebrows.

Fudge buckets of frogs.

"No! No… we…" I looked at Gran, glaring at her to help me cover, but she just sat there trying to cover her own giggling. A glance at Jen showed she wasn't going to be much more help either. Mothering. It's not for the weak or the slow-witted. "It's an adult thing. You'll understand someday." Ah, man. Childless people didn't give that excuse enough credit. She nodded like that was the answer to the universe and went back to surveying the dessert options. Whew.

"Maybe you should encourage your mother to judge some eating contests," Jen told her.

That was it. I kicked her hard under the table. No sex jokes around my child. She was never having sex. I was never going to have to have the sex talk. She was going to stay my baby forever. Denial, table of one.

"Nah, that sounds like they might get crumbs in the bed. Mommy and I ate cookies in her bed once, and the crumbs were itchy." She reached out and pulled a chocolate cake to her plate, carefully sliding it from the tray with precise movements.

I watched it all in horror, contemplating how much damage I might have just done to my child. She seemed okay. And how much did anyone remember about being seven, anyway? She was probably fine.

Oh, snickerdoodles.

"So... About school..." I interrupted, trying to remember any pertinent conversation that would get us away from 'eating' and 'bed.' "Umm... how are your teachers?" Hailey looked up from her cake, her fork dropping down to rest on the plate.

"Fine. I don't have any homework."

Wait. A. Minute. "Sweet pea?"

"Yes?"

"You know that you lie like me, right?" Repeaters. Over-sharers. We started lying and words just fell out. Kind of like the sex conversation of thirty seconds ago. Hailey's innocent face morphed as she dropped back in her chair, her arms crossed over her chest.

"I don't wanna read it."

"Hmm. Can I get a proper noun to go with that sentence?" I asked, but Hailey just looked at me with her eyebrows furrowed and her head cocked. At least I had confused her out of a complete rebellion. "What don't you want to read?" I clarified.

"Charlotte's web."

Okay. I think I was missing something.

"But sweetie, you already read that book."

"Yes. But she's making me do it again."

Okay… "And she's testing you on your knowledge tomorrow?"

"No."

"Then why don't you just…" Oh no. I couldn't tell my child to lie. One, she was bad at it. Two, that was bad parenting. "… skim it tonight? That way you can say you read it again, but don't have to go through it word for word?" She thought this over, and I could tell that I won because her arms dropped, and she went back to eating.

I also knew she still wasn't happy with my answer by the fact that she didn't verbally agree. Just ate her cake. Frankly? Today I was taking that as a win.

"So tell me, dears, how long are you two planning to hide here?" Gran asked with a smile. I looked at Jen, who sent a panicked glance at the door before turning back to Gran.

"You need some help to get ready for the Sewing Circle?" Jen asked.

It was at Alice's house tonight, but I knew Gran had promised to bring some food. Gran's eyes widened at the question and she looked away at Aunt Helen before she looked back at us.

I followed her gaze to where Aunt Helen was standing with Gladys, Dorothy, and some of the other girls from the Sewing Circle. They were all gathered around my aunt, and they seemed to be passing something between them. What were they doing?

"Lark, what are your plans tomorrow?" Gran asked, interrupting my focus.

"I have to drop off Hailey in the morning, get a few rides in, and then meet Connor for the tour of Barrow Bay and dinner," I replied, still trying to get a good look at what the ladies were doing. The way Gran kept moving to be in between me and them made me extra suspicious.

"And Connor is this new vet?" Gran asked, shaking her head at me. "I don't know what Brecken will think about that."

"That he doesn't care?" I snapped. Really. It wasn't going to happen. Not after today. I didn't care about his dog rescue story. Much. She should just get over it.

Gran looked at her phone, then looked back up at us with a smile. "So, you girls wanted to hide at my house for a few hours, right?"

Jen and I looked at each other, and then down at our phones. I had no idea what messages Jen had, but I had two from John, asking me to bring Jen out, and one from Brecken asking if we could talk. Yep. I was good with us hiding for a little while longer.

"Thanks, Gran."

CHAPTER 8

I let Gran drive us over to the Sewing Circle, despite a nagging feeling that it was a bad idea not to have an escape plan. Okay, it was less of a nagging feeling and more past experience, but Gran made a big deal about it, so we caved. Leaving Hailey with my uncle, the group of us, which included Aunt Helen, Jen, Gran, and me, all piled into her car with the food we had made that afternoon and drove the half a block to Alice and Benny's house.

Much like him, Benny's house was unassuming. It looked like any other house: simple green grass greeted the curb with sharp, well-maintained corners and the stucco was a flavor of beige that blended well with the others in the neighborhood. Clean lines and bland statements, the house was ordinary at first glance. All that changed, however, once inside. I remember the first time I came through those doors, expecting more beige, or maybe a rebel gray or two. But I had forgotten the purple-haired goddess that Benny married.

The floor was marble. Real Italian marble. I knew this because when my shoes hit it the first time, I slipped and had a close up viewing via landing on my behind.

One would think, for all the extra expense, Italian marble would have a softer landing. Or better grip for your shoe. Negative to both.

After the floor, the next thing that you took in was the swords. Accented nicely by the purple walls, there were a wide variety, from the large, heavy, knight swords from medieval movies, to the slim, curved, ninja ones. I had made the mistake of asking Benny where he got them, since there seemed to be a large variation in type. He had just looked down at his belly and asked me if he looked like someone who played with swords. I looked back, pointing out that Alice didn't look like it either, but one of them had to be a big fan because the leather on the cover had been recently oiled. I might be a little slow to notice things, but horse people always noticed the condition of leather.

He laughed and admitted they had done live-action role-playing when they were younger. *Live action role playing.* I had to look it up. It's when people pretend to fight. Well, and other things, but I got stuck on our town's Chief of Police swinging a sword with his wife cheering him on. Or the opposite. There was no way that Alice would let Benny fight without her wanting in on the action. I wanted pictures…. Just in case.

Gran had loaded us down with food, so I took careful steps as we headed to the kitchen, trying not to meet the floor again, this time covered in pasta. Gladys and Sallie Mae were already there, talking in the corner as we walked in. I did register some male voices in the living room, but Gran pushed us past too quickly for me to see who it was. I made a note to go back and say hi once we put everything down. I hadn't seen Benny in a while and wanted to catch up. Once unloaded, Alice was unpacking and unwrapping when Jen went stiff.

"Lark. Is Bobby working tonight?"

"The Uber driver? I don't know. Wait, doesn't he have classes with Missy?" I thought for a moment before I recalled her complaining about his cheese smell in class. "Yeah, I'm pretty sure he has class tonight."

"Damn it."

Well, now she had my complete attention. I moved closer to her so that I could see what she was looking at before asking, "Why?"

"Because I'm pretty sure Benny has the back door covered," Jen said with a long sigh.

I finally stood next to her and had an unobstructed view of the living room. The one my Grandmother didn't want me to see.

Smart woman.

"Nope. We're leaving. We can walk." I looked for my purse, but it was on the other side of the room. Too far. It would have to be abandoned.

Jen nodded and reached for her coat as we rushed for the front door.

"No! Leave it. We don't have time. Just run," I told her over my shoulder. Which was a bad plan. What was the first lesson we're taught as soon as we learned to walk? *Always* look where you are going. Because when I was fleeing cops with annoying questions and a possible date request, I was not a dainty little flower. No, when I ran into someone, going full break-neck walk, I ran them down, taking both myself and the hard body underneath me to the ground. I blame the tiles.

"Ouch," came a voice from underneath me.

My eyes had closed as I went down, squeezing tight, pretending that if I didn't see the floor it wouldn't hurt as hard. Which worked this time because my landing had been cushioned by the poor person below me.

"So now you're falling for me, huh? Does that mean I'm bumped up from annoying?" A cocky, low voice came from underneath me.

Wait. That was not Brecken.

Snickerdoodles. I wasn't supposed to care who I landed on. Or hope for it to be anyone specific, I guess. And especially not my unreliable, cover using, possible beau. Nope. I was footloose, fancy fre —

"Seriously. Are you going to get off?"

I glared. Yep, the view meeting my gaze was Special Agent Unimportant. Or was it Ass Hat? Had we decided yet?

"Was running into me really necessary?" I lied as I tried to figure out how to get off him without touching any more than I had to. It was official. Special Agent Ass Hat it was.

"You ran into me!" he protested as I lifted myself off. Brecken's hands were suddenly around my waist as I was jerked into the air and then placed on my feet, several feet back from Nicholas.

Wow. That was sexy.

Like, really sexy.

Anger forgotten, I couldn't help myself as I put a hand on his arm, feeling the muscles that I now knew must be there. Granted, I was in shape from exercising all day for my job and I was naturally skinny, even maybe a little on the waif side, as Jen liked to say, but I was still a tall girl. With a lot of muscles. And muscle weighed more than fat. At least that was what I told myself. He looked down at me as I touched his 'gun' and smiled. I felt him flex, the muscle jumping out into my hand, and I lost my breath.

Just gone.

It was in my lungs one moment and then poof. No air. I shouldn't have touched him. This was evil knowledge. As was the smile he had turned on me.

I really shouldn't have touched him.

I shouldn't have looked up at him.

I shouldn't have stared into his big blue eyes. Such pretty blue eyes.

His other arm, the one I wasn't fondling, tightened around me, and I couldn't stop my gaze from dropping to his lips as his touch sent tingling sensations through my body. Maybe Jen was right. Maybe it was a crime to never have tasted his —

"Lark!" A voice interrupted my thoughts, and I re-centered on the group.

"You okay, Lark?" Jen asked, a smirk hiding behind her compressed lips.

Yeah, biting into them didn't hide the smirk very well. I was pretty sure she was reading my mind. Hiding my hormones now.

"The women in this town are maniacs," Special Agent Ass Hat interrupted as he started getting up.

Jen, who was still standing close to him since she had been on my heels as we tried to run, frowned down at him for a second before taking a step forward. Right onto his foot, which he had been using to brace himself as he got up.

Back down he went, trying to escape the pain by moving backwards and instead losing his balance. "Ouch! What the hell?"

"Oh! I'm so sorry. Was that your foot?" She didn't even try to fake an innocent look as she walked past him, ignoring his angry look.

"I'm sorry, young man, but around here the men have manners." Gran came into the room, her gaze focused on Nicholas, with Sallie Mae and Alice following.

They looked like a little mafia. With white hair and wrinkles, but still ready to enact vengeance on the special agent that just called us maniacs. *Go Gran!*

"The men here don't swear in the presence of ladies." Gran eyed him, daring him to say we weren't ladies. On the surface, her face looked stern, but the twitch around her mouth told me she was amused.

"Is it horrible of me that I hope he says we aren't ladies?" I whispered to Brecken. That got me a smile and another squeeze on my hip.

Where his hand still rested. Oh my. There went my pulse rate.

What were we talking about?

Nicholas must have heard my comment because, after sending another glare my way, he said nothing as he got up from the floor. Benny, who had been watching everything from the sidelines with John, finally decided to intervene.

"Now, now, Special Agent. There's no need to get upset. Here, let's go back into the living room, where we'll be staying. All night. While you ladies talk out here." He sent a look at Alice that I couldn't interpret. Did he want her to do some digging? Or was he apologizing for the interruption? Nicholas sent us one last scowl before following Benny back into the living room. Brecken looked down at me before glancing back to the door.

"I need to go," Brecken whispered.

"So go." I didn't care. I hadn't grown so attached to his arm being around me in the past minute, that I knew it was going to hurt when he pulled it away. I hadn't. But I braced myself, just in case.

"I don't want to," he whispered, and I looked up. He was gazing down at me intently. So intently that I suddenly needed to swallow. What was he trying to say? I was just his cover. We both knew it, so why was he playing like it was more?

"Can we talk? Later?" His voice was low and rough.

"Yes." No! That was the hormones talking. Backpedal, backpedal. "No! I mean, we must go early. I don't know that we'll have time tonight." Okay, not the resounding no, my brain wanted me to say, but at least it wasn't a yes. Why did this man get to me?

His snort of laughter drew my eyes back to his. "That wasn't what you meant to say, was it?"

Oh.

Maybe that's why. He got me. My stupid. My sense of humor. And it never made him angry. No matter how idiotic the words coming out of my mouth were. That might be even sexier than his butt.

"No, but I'm going to go with it for now," I admitted before smiling back. *Maybe* I was being too jaded. *Maybe* he used the case as an excuse to see me, not the other way around. Maybe.

"Fine. I can wait for tomorrow. Can I see you in the morning?" He stared intently, with a smile that I was unused to seeing on his normally professional, stoic face.

Wait. Did Mr. Beat-Around-The-Bush-Until-The-Subject's-Dead just ask me out? Like straight-up out?

"Yes," I sighed. *Snickerdoodles.* "I mean NO!" My head dropped into my hands. *Way to play it cool, Lark.* "I have to drop Hailey off at her dad's." My voice came out a little mumbly through my hands.

"Can I come with?"

Yeah. I should have seen that one coming. And I had to answer it…

"Umm… sure?" Who was in control of my mouth, because it wasn't me. Then again, whoever it was might have had better answers than mine.

He smiled and gave me one last squeeze before joining the men in the living room. My eyes followed as I sat there and processed what just happened.

"I thought he was just here to use you as a cover?" Jen asked when we couldn't see him anymore.

"What just happened there?" Because I was still a little confused.

"I think he's taking you on a date after all. Or maybe you are taking him on a date? I mean, you are driving, so that would imply you being the takee—"

"Is that even a word?"

"Does it matter?"

"No. I guess not. And it's not a date. I don't take Hailey on dates with men. Oh, god. I don't introduce men to Hailey at all! Oh, no. I have to cancel. I can't do this." I started to run after Brecken, but Gran stopped me.

"She already knows him."

What the H-E-Double-hockey-sticks was she talking about? My arms crossed as I eyed Jen and Gran. I knew who the traitor was. That, and Jen hadn't babysat for me in a while. And she definitely had never volunteered to drive all the way to San Francisco two weeks ago to pick Hailey up from her dad's. Gran looked a little green but pulled herself to her full height and stuck her chin out.

"They met last time I went down there to pick Hailey up from her dad's. Brecken's sister lives close to his new barn."

I suddenly had the song of "It's A Small World" going around in my brain.

"So you, what… just bumped into him?" I growled. Her chin went up more. Oh, no. This was over the line.

I didn't care that he made me go weak at the knees. Wait. Where did that thought come from?

"No. We arranged to meet. It was supposed to be before, but he was running late. He's a policeman, Lark. He isn't a pedophile!"

"What if she gets attached? What happens in a few days when this case ends, and he goes home and forgets about us? Again?"

"Have you ever thought that might not happen? Or there might have been more happening in his life over the past month?"

"No. Because I deal in the real world. Where people don't just cooperate with all your manipulations!" I hissed, trying to keep my voice low so that the men in the other room didn't overhear it.

"You're right."

Wait. What?

"I shouldn't have kept the meeting once he was late, but, Lark, you need to talk to him. Stop seeing the world through only your filter and understand where he's coming from." Gran actually looked abashed for a second before she blasted past, back to her comfort zone of manipulation and pushing.

"No." Again, not the word I was looking for, but it worked, and I was done with the conversation. I turned and went into the kitchen, looking for an escape. Instead I found Dorothy eating all of Sally Mae's cookies. Well, that looked like a good reason to ignore my emotions for a while. Stuffing the emotions down where I didn't have to analyze them, I focused on Dorothy.

"I thought no one ate any cookies that Sallie Mae made," I commented as she stuck another one in her mouth. Jen sat down next to her and took one of the cookies with a sigh.

"Two of my grandsons want to be the General Manager at the hotel when I retire in a few months."

"Grandsons? Plural?" I asked. That wasn't going to be fun. Telling one relative that the other was better? That was worthy of cookie eating, even Sallie Mae's.

"Yep."

"You going to have two GMs?"

"Nope."

"Hire from the outside?" Jen offered, instinctively needing to help fix the situation.

"One of the grandsons is perfect. The other wants it more," Dorothy replied.

We all sat there, contemplating how Dorothy was going to choose between two of her family members. She took another cookie before turning to Jen, who also stuffed another cookie in her mouth. Not good.

"They found something?" Dorothy asked Jen around the cookie.

Not her best look.

"Yep," Jen replied and Dorothy nodded, like that made sense.

Was I missing something? Who were 'they'? And what did they find? And how did Dorothy know before I did?

"Was he working with Tony?"

Tony? As in Tony Harris? My ex-client's husband? Someone had better start explaining.

"Yep. It looks like my business partner was in on it from the start," Jen said as she took another cookie. This time breaking it into pieces, instead of putting it in her mouth. "These cookies are horrible."

She wasn't kidding. Gladys was a horrible baker. That's why I stopped when I saw Dorothy eating them. Only desperate people ate Gladys' cookies.

"Can anyone fill me in?" I asked, finding the container of cookies I made earlier and slipping them over. Dee took one with a grateful look and Jen snagged one with a nod.

"Tony has been one of my business partner's clients for years. Three months ago, the account was passed to me to get ready for my partner's retirement. Until I turned them in last month for insider trading."

Well, that was not good. At least, it sounded bad. And the FBI was here. Yep, I was leaning toward really bad.

"My old partner has been implicated as well. That's why Special Agent Ass Hat is here. With Brecken, who is the local contact for the San Francisco department where Tony and my partner live, and our local police. And since I had records in my office at home, everyone got to come out here and search. He's digging into our records, trying to find anyone else that could have been involved. And me."

"You?"

"Yep. He's trying to find the evidence on me. I could have a black heart, evidently."

"Have you ever noticed that these men are always trying to blame us?" I asked. They both quirked their eyebrows at me. Okay, I guess that wasn't clear. "When I found the leg, Brecken was convinced I was involved. Now, Special Agent Ass Hat is going after Jen."

"One, he thought that because of your address. They found it in—" Dorothy started to tell me before I interrupted.

"WHAT?"

"Yeah, that's why they were all over you for drug dealing. He found a paper with your address on it and a mention of drugs from San Fran."

Oh. He found my address, but really it was supposed to be Annie's address. We really needed to change one of the street names. That actually made more sense.

"Huh. Okay. What's number two?"

"Two, are you going to call him Special Agent Ass Hat the whole time? Doesn't that get tiring? It's super long. Wouldn't it be easier to just call him Nicholas? Or just Ass Hat?" Dee lifted an eyebrow at me, silently reproaching me for my immature name giving. She probably guessed it was a cover for the fact that I was horrible with names. Dee was too insightful like that.

Since she had a point, I looked at Jen, who shrugged her shoulders.

"Fine. Nic it is," I agreed.

"No! What if I was voting for Ass Hat? And why Nic? Can't we call him Nicholas?" Jen protested.

"If I can't call him by a nickname, then I certainly am not going to call him by his full name. It takes too long. And it isn't cool," I informed her.

"But Nic is too intimate. Like we're friends. We're *not* friends."

"I'm not saying his whole name because you're afraid you might like him more if we call him Nic." I did my best Jen eye roll at her and she gasped.

"I do not."

"Do too."

"Do not."

"Do too."

"Ok, unless you two are going to find a third and start going into the old Three Stooges routines, we need to stop this conversation now," Dorothy snapped at us. We both turned to her, then looked at each other.

"Do you think Hailey could…" Jen tapped her finger on her chin thoughtfully.

"We're not teaching my daughter to do slapstick comedy!"

"But it's a life skill!"

"Not in this life! Someone needs to take care of me when I'm old!"

CHAPTER 9

Brecken was at my door bright and early the next morning.

I greeted him, already dressed for the day, and two cups of coffee in. I didn't tell anyone that the reason I was up so early was because I had woken up at four AM, contemplating all the ways this could go wrong.

I did spend about ten minutes thinking of all the ways this could go right, but then I realized that the calendar I had bought last month with the policemen of San Francisco in it, shirtless, was on the counter. An hour later, my house was cleaner and completely sanitized of anything Brecken-related. I hoped.

"Hey. You want coffee?" I asked. Then stood there waiting for his answer, looking everywhere but at him. Because I was smooth like that.

"Sure."

I nodded before walking to the kitchen where Hailey was finishing up her breakfast.

"Brecken!" She greeted him with a wave and a happy smile.

I was not going to freak out about this. Hailey was allowed to know people. Even male people. I could do this.

"Hailey! How's school going?" His smile looked real and warm.

Was he a kid person? Oh no. My ovaries might explode. That's not fair.

"Good. Did Mom tell you I'm going to a festival?"

"I'm sorry. Try that again?" I turned to look at her, ready to pounce. No drug festivals!

"Not that festival," she said with a shake of her head. "Mom's unhappy because I went to the Blues festival a few weeks ago and there was a drug arrest. Can you tell her it's not a big thing?"

"If your mother says no, she has good reasons." He nodded in support of my decision.

Good choice, buddy. His sister had trained him well.

"Don't even try the lip. No." I got the lower lip anyway, but I was able to resist. As I had since she started being able to talk back. It became less cute when she started telling me how mean I was. "Can you go get your overnight bag?" I waited until she was out of the room to turn to Brecken. "How bad was that festival?"

"This is the one that happened the last time I was here?"

I nodded.

"Let's put it this way. Several guys got promoted from that drug bust."

Oh god.

"Asking for a friend: would a jury acquit a mother who killed her child's father for letting her go to a festival where there was a major drug bust?"

"And my answer is the same as last time. It works better if you don't tell a cop your plans. You have to think it really hard."

"Maybe I should start dating a lawyer," I muttered under my breath.

"They don't help you get rid of parking tickets," Brecken offered back with a smirk.

"That would be a better sales pitch if we gave out parking tickets in Barrow Bay. I haven't had a parking ticket, well, ever."

"I know. I checked."

"You know, reminding me that you pulled my records when you were investigating me is a turn off." I frowned at him, but he just smiled at me and got up to meet Hailey by the door. Pouring fresh coffee into two go-cups, I followed.

I had a feeling I was going to need a lot of coffee. In fact, I don't know if I *could* make enough coffee for this.

The ride out to Blake's new barn was quiet, at least between Brecken and me. Hailey was a completely different story. Now, I liked to think of myself as a good mom. I didn't swear around my child, well, in real swear words. I helped her with her homework, no matter how many issues I had with it. And I let her play her flute in the house without taking it to the barn and letting the horses trample it.

So, a pretty good parent.

I did let one of her classmate's parents use Twice to have an unfortunate violin accident, though. I even videoed the mare ripping the violin to shreds. I was a firm believer in parents helping other parents. And that violins were evil.

Either way, I liked to think of myself as a good parent. But an hour and a half of seven-year-old babble from my daughter and I was numb. I felt battle-tired as I pulled the truck into Blake's driveway. How could something that cute talk about nothing for that long? And expect answers? No, I don't know why the sky was blue, honey. Oh? You do? Great. Let's hear about it for thirty minutes. I loved that.

But what was worse was that Brecken *was* loving it. Like actually enjoying talking about nothing in a loop. Smiling at her questions, taking time to listen to her answers and responding. I would have been less surprised if a unicorn jumped in front of my truck. In fact, I was surprised we didn't crash with how often I was staring at them with my mouth hanging open. He got my sense of humor. He could talk to a seven-year-old for almost two hours without snapping or rolling his eyes once. Would kidnapping him and making a run for Vegas be wrong? There were all those stories about people that go there and get accidentally married. It had to be easy, right? A little alcohol… some bad decisions… boom.

No. That was bad. Getting married so that I had another person to listen to my child talk was a bad reason. Tempting, though.

I glanced over at his face.

Very tempting.

No! No. I was only supposed to be talking about *maybe* letting him have another chance at a date.

Not kidnapping him.

Or marrying. That would be… overreacting. I was still watching their conversation when we pulled into Blake's driveway and stopped in front of his house. A bleached-blonde stood by the door, her boobs covered by slips of fabric. I had concerns about them not being up to the challenge. Who wore something like that on a Saturday morning? Slipping the truck into park, I continued to take in the picture in front of me.

"Who's that?" Brecken asked, his eyebrows meeting his hair line as his eyes continued down.

Was he kidding me with this? Wasn't he in this car to try to get me? Because he was failing.

"Where, exactly, does she think she's going? Because I'm pretty sure the stri—" He cut himself off when I cleared my throat and gestured behind me. "Um… clubs are closed at this time of day."

Forgiven. He was absolutely forgiven.

"What's a club?" Hailey asked from the back.

Snickerdoodles.

"A place where adults… go to…" Hook up. Get some. Drink. Be stupid. Not one of the sarcastic answers that came to my mind could be told to a child. I shot Brecken a dirty look for getting me into this.

"Meet up with other adults," Brecken finished for me, shooting me a victorious grin.

Yeah, I guess not being sarcastic might have been helpful right then. That was a much easier, more child-appropriate answer.

"Why?" she challenged.

Hah! I waited for him to give her the answer.

"Don't you like talking with your friends at school?"

"Sure."

"Same thing. Only adults don't have school, so they go to bars."

"But mommy says that school is like work. Why don't adults just talk with their friends at work?"

"Because not everyone works with their friends," he answered, turning in his seat to look at her straight on.

"Okay." She smiled at him and unbuckled her seatbelt. I got out to rush around to open the door. She jumped down, ignoring my hand and ran towards the door yelling for Blake. He came out of the house at her call, greeting her with a hug and a big smile.

"She's amazing. You are so lucky," Brecken commented as we both watched her run to her dad's arms. Blake grabbed her and swung her up in the air in circles a few times making her laugh. Their blond hair matched, both light dirty blond to my darker browns, and she had his strong chin and big expressive eyes. Separately, they were both pretty. Together? Knock outs.

"I am. I don't know how Blake and I have done it, but she's the best."

"She has a great mother." He smiled down at me and my heart took off in my chest. Oh goodness. His eyes should be illegal. It was so unfair.

"Hey, Lark! Thanks for bringing her down this weekend," Blake called out as he carried Hailey back over to the car, his six-foot-two frame easily carrying her. I stared at them for a little longer because I missed carrying her. Being able to sweep her up into my arms and hold her close as she snuggled in. There was no feeling like it. Even riding. I missed it.

"Anytime, Blake." *Please don't take me up on that.* "Who's your friend?" I asked, gesturing to Double-D, who had stayed on the porch for the reunion.

"Not my friend. She wants to be yours, though," he said, a frown spreading across his face.

"*My* friend?" I didn't know if I wanted any more friends. On the other hand, I could use more clients. I took another look at her. The fabric I struggled to call a dress was expensive, I thought. Maybe designer. I tried to get more information but gave up. Jen would've known better. I guess it might be worth listening to her more when she talked about her designer obsession. The lady, because calling a client Double-D would be a bad idea, took my assessment as an invitation to come over and I decided to give her the benefit of the doubt. Maybe she was uber rich and had a dressage horse that needed to be trained. You never knew.

Customer service smile on.

"Hello. You must be Lark." She had a smooth voice, pleasant and practiced.

I wasn't the only one in customer service mode. My question was why.

"Yes. And you are?"

"Tiffany."

I waited for a last name and she just stared at me. Well, okay then.

"Is that just Tiffany? Like Cher?" Hmm. On the next sentence I might try less sarcasm and more customer service. Lucky for me, she just laughed.

"Tiffany Harris."

Well, that didn't sound good. I shot Blake a look, and he turned around and ushered our child to somewhere else, presumably some place free of revealing dresses and talk about dead horses.

"Any relation to Tony Harris?" I glanced at Brecken, who had lost his relaxed expression and had put on his police face. Too bad. I liked him relaxed.

"Unfortunately." Her face scrunched up, like she had tasted something sour. Hmm. I didn't think she liked him. "Sister," she said, glancing at Brecken for a moment before refocusing on me.

I waited for her second glance at the Captain America look-alike beside me, but it never came.

Interesting.

"And you wanted to talk with me?" I clarified. Because I didn't know why anyone would want to talk to me. Unless she had a dressage horse. *Please have a dressage horse.*

"I talked with Connor this morning. The labs confirmed that there was a small amount of Oleander in Bon Voyage's system," Tiffany told me, studying me from head to shoes. "I asked around and found out you would be here this morning."

I didn't kill him. Thank god. Even though I had guessed that he had been poisoned, it was nice to have confirmation. But what did she want? "And you decided to meet me here?"

"I came here to answer questions. It was significantly closer." She looked me in the eye and raised her chin.

I didn't understand. My questions?

"What questions am I supposed to ask you?" I asked, raising my hands up to emphasize my cluelessness. Did she mean Brecken? How would she have known he was going to be here?

"How about Bon's training? You had questions."

"How did you know that?" I was starting to feel like I was in a Bond movie. She was certainly dressed for it.

"Good guess work?" She shrugged at me, leaning against the truck, unconcerned that her dress was getting dirty.

I couldn't help my stare. My truck was a work truck. It had layers of dirt so deep I had to take it through the car wash twice sometimes. But she didn't care. I was stuck on that. I cared, and it was my truck. Plus, I was usually just as dirty. But I still *cared*. How did she not care?

"Since the divorce papers were issued, Abby and I have been working to negate Tony's influence on my company. Switching to a trainer Tony couldn't intimidate was one of the first steps. We might have been a little late on that." She frowned and I could see pain in her eyes. Abby wasn't the only one hurt by Bon's loss.

Emily had definitely missed the boat thinking that Abby and Tiffany didn't care about the horse. Bon had two people in his life that cared a great deal about him, even if they didn't show it in the way we trainers expected.

"If it was Tony, he snuck onto my property to poison Bon. Moving him earlier wouldn't have helped," I pointed out, trying to reduce her guilt. Also, I need to look into getting cameras. As soon as possible. I didn't know why I hadn't done it already, although the thought of having an issue twice in a town like Barrow Bay had seemed unlikely. "When were the divorce papers served?"

"Two days before the move."

Fudge Buckets. That explains the separate cars at the animal hospital.

"Was that before they found out about the insider trading?"

"No. The SEC informs you when you're being investigated. That was the last straw for Abby. She couldn't take having her name tied to his anymore."

I looked over at Brecken, still confused by why he hadn't spoken up. Or why I was in the middle of this conversation at all. Well, if I was going to lead, I was going to get the information I cared about. Mainly, why I failed in the three days I had him to find the horse he should have been.

"You were following his training?" I asked.

"Yes. Abby and I didn't have the time to follow the daily training routine, but we were active in following up with Emily and going to the shows." She smiled at my change in questions.

Good. Not as out of it as Emily had claimed. "When did you notice the change in him?"

"The change? You mean when he stopped performing as well? Four months ago. Right after Emily lost her own private mount. Frankly, since she lost that horse, she hasn't been the same trainer, either."

"What do you mean?" Less applicable, but I was always down for a little horse gossip. Not one of my better characteristics.

"Well, she lost him about a week before the first bad show. Colic, I think? Anyway, she lost him and that whole show was off. She was stressed and short with us and Bon. She was so tense you could have tapped her on the shoulder and sent her jumping into the sky. It was no surprise that they didn't show well. We wrote it off as bad timing, but the next show was even worse."

"Did she talk to you about checking him? Doing a full lameness test at the vet hospital? Maybe an MRI or x-rays?"

"We had a lameness exam done by Connor, but he didn't find anything. Emily insisted he was fine, and she just needed to put more miles under the saddle." Tiffany frowned. "That was when we started looking around for another trainer."

Miles under the saddle. Interesting turn of phrase. And very accurate to the horse I sat on. But I remembered such an amazing horse when I saw him six months ago. Could I have been that wrong? Maybe I was remembering a different horse?

Or maybe it was a regression? That did happen. It felt like regressions happened each time I tried to move a horse up a level. But this felt like more.

Then again, maybe I should stop obsessing about my own failings and get back to the crime.

"How long have you and Abby Harris been lovers?" Brecken asked.

Thank goodness Brecken finally took over. I had no idea what else to ask her and…

WHAT?

Tiffany smiled at him.

"Detective Brecken Wilson, I presume?" She waited for his nod before continuing.

His lips compressed into a line at her knowledge, and I suppressed my need to dance around. He didn't like it when other people researched him. HAH!

"Fifteen years. Soon after Abby and Tony got married. We were best friends in college, and I was how they met. Abby is bi, and at first Tony and she were so in love. Then," she sighed, "business wasn't good to my brother. He shouldn't have been thrown into our family company like he was. My father should have seen that Tony wouldn't be able to handle it. Soon, the Tony that Abby and I had known was gone and the Tony of today was there in his place. Abby grew to hate him. We became closer in our shared frustration of his behavior. Too close, I guess. I… don't make my preferences known in my world. It was easier to just let Abby stay married than to break the scandal. That changed with the recent information."

"But she flirted with men," I blurted out. Oh, my goodness. I didn't just tell someone that their long-term girlfriend was flirting with other men. I had only seen it at a few shows, or events when I lived down here, but people talked, and I wasn't that out of the community. Please tell me I didn't just do that.

"Yep. Abby might be in love with me, but she still loves to flirt with men. She loves the chase, the compliments, the appreciation. Until the end. Then she comes home to me."

"That doesn't bother you?" Because I was ready to do bodily harm to Brecken for just checking out Tiffany. Not that we're dating. Because we were not. And if the rage in my soul from the reminder of how he checked her out was any indication, we weren't going to be anytime soon. Huh. Didn't know I was a jealous person. I hadn't even noticed Blake's wandering eye. I'd had other things to do, horses to train, clients to teach, a child to raise.

Wow.

I hadn't cared what Blake did.

It made me uncomfortable, but I realized I might have to accept some responsibility for the divorce myself. I had never felt as possessive of Blake as I did of Brecken right now. Never. Well… that should have been a sign.

"No. I already share her with my brother. This is already messed up enough without cheating and jealousy."

"Good point." At least they all acknowledged how messed up the situation was.

"Do you think that he killed the horse?" Brecken asked.

"Yes. No doubt in my mind."

"Any evidence?"

"Not a thing." She shook her head to emphasize the words.

I found my gaze dropping to watch as the dress came precariously close to flashing us.

"Do you have any other questions?" she asked.

"Did you know about the insider trading?" Brecken threw out quickly.

"Ah-ah, Detective. Those questions would need to go to my lawyers. Because this conversation didn't happen." She stopped leaning against the truck and absently brushed the dirt from her dress.

"Why didn't this conversation happen?" I whispered to Brecken, but Tiffany overheard and answered.

"Because my lawyers would have a fit if they knew I was talking to you, much less Detective Hot Stuff over there." She flashed him an appreciative smile, and I went cold. "I try to not anger the people who keep me out of jail. They might miss an important detail. Also, my brother and his attorney would be livid."

"It's Detective Captain America to you." I couldn't believe I said that out loud. To a lesbian. I may have been out of the loop for several years, but I was still pretty sure that being a lesbian meant that she couldn't be less interested in my man. His man. Him. Brecken. Whatever!

Tiffany just laughed at me, her laughter light, engaging and practiced. Real people chortle, you overly pretty woman-liking... person. I was struggling to find things to dislike about this woman. She was cool, gorgeous, well-dressed, rich, and thought I was funny. Jealousy was irrational.

"You two are so cute. How long have you been dating?" she asked, still giggling quietly.

"We haven't," I snapped.

Brecken, who had decided to flirt with danger, smiled down at me like I was... like I was *cute!* I was not *cute*.

Wait.

Okay, maybe I was cute. I don't wear enough makeup to rate hot these days. I glanced at Tiffany's fabric. Or wear clothing that hid nothing. But he didn't have to agree with her.

I lost my train of thought there...

Ah! Yes! He should not be looking at me like my protests were cute. They were denials. He should be hurt. Crying. Throwing himself on the floor in pain.

Oh god.

It's official.

I was completely crazy. Maybe I should just call up the loony bin now and turn myself in.

"We're going out on a date today," Brecken answered for me when my insanity kept me silent for too long.

"No, we're not," I snapped, crossing my arms in front of me.

Tiffany laughed in the background, clearly enjoying our debate.

"Lark. I'm sorry I let you think that I was here for the case—"

"You *are* here for the case. You said, and I quote, 'I'm not here for you,' end quote." I even did the little hand quotes for emphasis. "Were you lying then?"

"No… It's just… You are…" He took a deep breath and released it with a long hiss. "Frustrating. You are frustrating."

"Oh, let my heart be still." I glared at him, my body going rigid with anger.

"He means you are frustrating him, not that you are frustrating," Tiffany clarified.

We both turned to face her, shocked that she was still there. And that she had the lady balls to step into the middle of the conversation. I mean, we knew she was there, but we had forgotten that she was there.

"I'm guessing you don't do a lot of relationships?" she asked Brecken, who joined me in crossing his arms over his chest and glaring.

He really didn't like being around someone who was as insightful as he was. I was torn between staying angry at him and being delighted at watching him squirm.

"It's none of your business," he snapped.

"He means no," I answered for him. Still think I'm *cute*, fudge monkey?

"That's what I thought. He's too attractive to have much trouble finding girls to feed his ego. Probably don't hear the word 'no' much either, with him being a policeman and all."

"That's what I thought!" I told her, uncrossing my arms and relaxing.

"You tell him 'no' and he likes it. He just doesn't know what to do with it."

Okay, I guess I could see what she was saying.

"But what am I supposed to do while he figures it out? I'm not a wait-around kind of gal," I said, making sure nothing in my body acknowledged the man standing next to me.

"Well, for starts, I would enjoy your date with Connor tonight." She flashed Brecken a smirk at his glower. "He's certainly excited about it. Don't wait. Have fun. Sow a few oats. You can't make up other people's minds for them. They have to do it. *You* do *you*."

I was not going to mention that 'me doing me' consisted of peanut M&Ms, Netflix, and wine. She obviously thought I had a life. I wouldn't want to correct it.

She smiled at whatever she saw on our faces and with that, turned and walked away, her left butt cheek peeking out of the fabric with every step.

"So, I know that lesbians don't dress a certain way, because sexual preference doesn't affect clothing choices, but... what's up with that dress?" I asked Brecken quietly. He didn't have a kid. He might be more up on trends than me.

"I *can* make up my mind," he stated firmly.

He can make up his mind about the dress? OH! Oh… Wait. I didn't want to have this conversation anymore. If he could make up his mind, he was going to want a decision from me, too. Panicked deflection.

"So, I guess we're not going to talk about the dress."

"I know what I want." He took a step closer.

Why was my heart racing? "That's okay, I'll just process the dress on my own. No need for your help."

"I *know* what I *want*." Another step.

"Fine! You know what you want. Good for you. I don't." Well, that was a lie… kind of. Running away sounded good. What if he told me he was all in? What if he told me he *wasn't* all in? I was gasping for air.

"Lark?" His face was in front of me suddenly, no longer confident. Now he was more concerned.

"You terrify me," I gasped. Yep. This was how I got a man. By arguing with him, telling him no, and then having a panic attack before he could tell me if he was interested or not. I truly was a sexy beast.

"Good. Because you frustrate the hell out of me." He chuckled and led me back behind the truck where we weren't in the view of the house. "She was right. No one really tells me no. Not like you do."

Well. That was… heart-stoppingly romantic. Ok, maybe not the words, but the meaning really worked for me.

"Everyone finds me strange. Only you find me amusing," I whispered back, my emotions demanding I tell him one of my truths in return.

"Everyone loves you. Do you know that when I came back, Benny talked with me for three hours about not texting you more while I was home? Three hours, Lark. Not one piece of work done." Wow. For him, that must have been torture. "But I sat through it. Because everyone loves you."

"Laura didn't." *Sweet cheese and crackers.* Sometimes I want to slap myself for not controlling my mouth. Brecken laughed.

"Laura liked you fine. She just didn't like that Bryan liked you more. Everyone likes you. *Everyone.*" He put extra emphasis on the last word, and I felt like it was a message for me. Was he saying that he was included in that 'everyone'? My legs went limp.

"Blake didn't." OH MY GOD. Why was I still arguing this? *Kiss him already.*

Oh god. No. I shouldn't do that. I just needed to breathe. No panicking. Panicking would be bad. Panicking might lead to bad decisions. Like kissing him. Or not kissing him. When did I stop knowing which was the bad idea?

"Blake's an idiot." He leaned closer to me and lifted my chin up. I was still a little gaspy, but his eyes locking on mine helped. I was struggling to put two thoughts together when he looked at me like that. His gaze made me forget how much of a bad idea this was.

He moved a little closer, and every nerve lit up.

He was going to kiss me.

I was going to let him.

Heat surged through me, and I felt a little lightheaded, but I let my body drift towards his. I watched him leaning down, the arm not at my chin slipping around my waist to pull me closer. When he was centimeters from my mouth, he stopped and waited.

Why?! Why was he waiting? He needed to kiss me already!

"Please tell me you want this," he whispered, his lips brushing mine as he spoke.

Oh. OH. Ohhhh. Consent. Got it.

"Yes." His lips covered mine before I even finished the word, and suddenly the world stopped.

His movements were tentative, slow, like he was savoring each second. Maybe he expected me to push him away, but I didn't have enough fear to fight this anymore. I let him explore, opening my mouth and letting him take everything before I kissed him back. That was when the change happened. My mild-mannered detective, who didn't know how to handle someone who said no, morphed. The hand that had been holding my chin at the right angle for his kiss, was suddenly wrapped in my hair, pulling me even closer to him, like he wanted to eliminate any distance between us. I reached out to grab his shoulders and his arm slipped from my waist to my butt, pulling me so close I was flush against his body.

Well. Hello there, soldier.

"Lark!" A voice came from the front of the truck.

Brecken pulled me a little tighter, which was impressive since I could already feel every inch of him.

"Lark! Is everything — shit." Blake came around the corner of the truck and then threw his hand over his eyes.

I debated if Blake was close enough to kick, but when I figured that I would be several inches short, I settled for uncoiling myself from Brecken. Who was not taking Blake's appearance well either. Brecken looked like he was alternating between pain and anger. At least that was my guess from the narrowed eyes and tightness around his mouth that came and went.

"What did you need, Blake?" I asked with a sigh.

"Is this for my benefit? You are angry about me bringing all my girlfriends around, and so you bring home… him?" He finally pulled the hand down from his eyes and put them on his hips. Like he was the parent, and I was some wayward teenager caught making out with a boy.

Had he always been an egomaniac? How had I missed that all these years?

"No, Blake. I don't make out with people to get back at you. I didn't even bring him. He invited himself." Too much information. Oops.

"And you let him? You don't let people do anything you don't want."

Well, that was true.

"Okay, I wanted him to come." Brecken flashed me a naughty grin, and I had to work to ignore him so I could focus on Blake. Also, why do all the men in my life have names that start with B? Wait. Connor. Score. I got one that broke the pattern.

Conner. *Fudge buckets.* I needed to figure out what I wanted to do about him. I was pretty sure that kiss meant… something. Or did it? The media kept going on and on about the 'hook-up' generation. Maybe I shouldn't count my chickens, and all that. Hmm… that probably would be more accurate if I said, 'count my cocks before they hatch.'

Oh my god. I couldn't believe I just thought that.

I couldn't even look at Brecken after that thought.

"So, you could throw your new man in my face?" Blake was still going on about this indignity.

Shiitake mushrooms. Did he really think that everything in my life was about him?

"No—" I started only to be cut off.

"Because I know the divorce was hard on you and you have had trouble getting over me…"

WHAT? I was having trouble getting over what he *did*. I had no trouble getting over him. Egomaniac wasn't strong enough for this man's ego.

"… but there was no call to find some actor to come here and play your boyfriend."

Actor? He thought Brecken was an actor? I looked at Brecken. Okay. I could see that. I had to look away before Blake could see the smile on my face. I made sure it was completely under control before I turned to face him.

"You're right. I did this all for your sake. Brecken is just an actor. What's it that you do when you aren't playing poor divorcee's fake boyfriends, again?"

"Detective." Brecken was on to my game and had his most intimidating police face on when he turned to face my ex head-on. "I normally work in the area, too. I'll definitely look forward to seeing you around."

"Normally?" Evidently Blake wasn't ready to back down. Or he hadn't caught onto the threat. It was a toss-up.

"I'm on vacation in Barrow Bay for the week. I was working a case there a few weeks ago and I found that I left something behind I couldn't live without."

WHAT? I turned to face Brecken, only to find him staring at me. Did he... Could he mean... I couldn't breathe again.

"I'm leaving. I'll see you when you drop Hailey off on Sunday. And no festivals with drug busts." I needed to get in the truck and think about what was just said. *Don't stop me now.*

"Got it. Oh! And Lark?"

"What?" I said don't stop me.

"I told everyone that he was lying. So did Christy and her trainer. You still have friends out here. No one is taking Tony seriously."

Oh. *Shiitake mushrooms.* My job. Yeah, I should care about that. I wanted to say, 'yes, Christy's awesome,' but Blake sticking up for me was too nice. Sneaky man.

"Thank you, Blake. See you Sunday night."

He nodded and Brecken followed me to the truck door, opening mine before helping me into the truck, which was incredibly romantic.

And awkward. Normally I just throw myself up, hoisting one leg onto the seat and then using the leverage to pull the rest of my body in. With Brecken there I couldn't do that without looking, well, awkward. But I also didn't know how to accept help. My muscle memory kept trying to force me into getting in like normal, but now my hand was trapped. And I didn't want to push off his hand because that wasn't what ladies do. I didn't think.

In the end, I managed to hop in, thanks to my abnormal height, without letting Blake know that I was having issues. Brecken, however, was a lost cause. He had caught on to my logistical confusion and only barely managed to keep his snickers under his breath. His eyes crackled with laughter that he tried not to let out, however. He seemed to realize that I wanted to seem, well, less 'me' in front of my ex and was trying to cover for me, if badly… Barely keeping it together, he went around the front of the truck, using it to block Blake's view, before jumping into the passenger's side.

"Hold it in." I ordered as I turned the truck back on and shifted into drive. And we did. Until the end of the driveway. Then I had to pull to the side of the road.

And we laughed.

CHAPTER 10

So, you ready to talk yet?" Brecken asked once we hit the freeway. We had both stopped laughing, and he had waited until I was relaxed before he asked me the questions I had been avoiding for a day now.

"Sure. Why not?" I wasn't going to verbalize all the reasons going through my mind on why I didn't want to have this conversation. Playing it cool.

"I *did* come here for the case."

Really? That was where he wanted to start?

"Wow, Brecken. You really know how to woo a girl."

"Can you stop interrupting me to be snarky?"

"I think you know that answer by now." I glanced over at him with a head shake. "I would if I could, but I can't, so I shan't."

"I didn't pin you as a *Big Bang Theory* fan."

"Just because I don't have a college degree doesn't mean I'm dumb." I threw a flat look at him to let him know my thoughts on that.

"I'm starting to see that."

"Starting?" I couldn't stop my voice getting higher as I said it. Wherever this conversation was going, it wasn't getting there well.

"Turn of phrase?" he offered, wincing at my angry expression.

"When was that wooing starting? Because I'm feeling substantially less inclined."

"I was kind of hoping we were over the wooing portion of this. You know, after the kiss and all." His eyes were kind of wide by the end of his statement.

Were we? Was I okay with that?

"Nope."

"Nope?"

"Nope, I need more wooing."

"What, exactly, constitutes wooing? I haven't brushed up on my old-time courting techniques recently."

I glared at him but had to stop and think about that. What did I want? I couldn't recall any man asking me that before. What I wanted out of a relationship. It completely flummoxed me.

"Dates," I finally offered. "Texting. Every day. Ooh and a 'good morning' text every morning. I had a roommate once whose boyfriend did that. It was so romantic." I looked over at him to see how he took that, only to find him just staring at me. Then it hit me. "You were joking, weren't you?" Well, that was disappointing.

"I was, but I'm finding that I like having a list. Lists are good. I can do lists." He was nodding over and over as he pulled out his phone and looked at me again. "Text messages every morning and dates. Got it. What else?"

He was serious. Was I?

Oh god. I was. I was going to do this.

"Status. I don't like being up in the air, or not knowing what I am, or who I am to you… or, really, anything. I like knowing things."

"Nosy. Got it."

I stuck my tongue out at him, but continued my list anyway. "I want to keep dating other people, too. Until…" I knew he wasn't going to disappear. I couldn't say that. Could I? I glanced over at him and then back to the road.

"Until you know I'm sticking around." He grimaced before looking away. "I should explain that."

Yeah, that would be a good idea.

"Only if you want to," I lied.

"I—" He stopped and tightened his hands on his notebook. "I separate things in my life. My work, well, it doesn't mix well with life."

I could see that. John and Judy had a rule where he never talked about his work at home.

"I compartmentalize my work, and my family and… well, that's all I have right now, but everything is separate. Or it was." He took a deep breath. "I moved here for my sister."

And… not where I thought this was going.

"My family doesn't talk about it much. It's hard for her, and none of us like people in our business. It's even harder for me because—" He pretended to be very interested in something on the road for a second before continuing. "She married a cop. Who beat her. And then made false complaints to keep her in the area or she would lose custody of their son."

Another cop hurt his sister. I glanced at his stiff posture. He had to have taken that hard, harder than if it had been someone else. He probably felt doubly betrayed. First by his brother-in-law and second as a cop who lived to uphold the law.

"The second time he showed up at her door after the divorce and beat her up, my family packed our stuff and moved. The next time he knocked on her door, intending to smack her around a little more, I was there. And the next. And the next. This last month we finally sued for full custody. Full custody without any visitation rights. We have enough evidence of wrong-doings, but it will be a little longer until the court date."

I suddenly felt the need to go buy a gun. Or go borrow Nancy's, my neighbor's. She couldn't see well enough to use it, anyway. And she would probably give me an alibi while I was at it. These were the things I loved about my small town.

"We want to move away from him, and my family has been looking around." He put his phone down and carefully straightened out something on his pants. Something I was pretty sure didn't exist. "I used this case as an excuse to come back to Barrow Bay before…" He hesitated and looked at his pants again.

Oh my god. He was going back East. Back home to where he was from. I was getting dumped. Again.

Couldn't he have told me this before we kissed? Before I knew what I was missing out on? Because, to be honest, Brecken was a really good kisser. Or it had been a really long time. Or I had been with a really bad kisser. I was getting distracted.

"… Before we decided anything. Lark?"

Another hesitation. These waits were killing me.

"Whatever," I muttered.

"Lark, we're thinking… whatever? Did you just say 'whatever'?" Well, he wasn't hesitating anymore. He also looked like I was crazy.

"Yes." I glanced at him from the corner of my eye then back at the road. He looked shocked. Complete with eyebrows raised and mouth hanging. "I'm guessing that was the wrong answer."

His mouth snapped shut, and he seemed to be thinking hard before a smile broke out on his face.

"You think I'm telling you that I'm leaving."

Well, yeah.

"You're not?"

"Nope. I'm going to stay in San Francisco for now. Then we'll see what happens after that."

Snickerdoodles. I had forgotten about that. Completely. I felt like my world just flipped upside down. Completely.

"But you're thinking about moving."

"Yes."

"Where does that leave us?" Now it was my turn to hesitate. I wanted a commitment. Without actual commitment. "I need things spelled out. With terms."

"Do you need a legal document, too? Signatures with witnesses?" He lifted an eyebrow at me, with a knowing look.

"Contract sounds good, although I don't know about the witnesses…" Oh god. That was a joke. About marriage. Where did the air go?

"Lark. It was a joke. Just a joke. Please don't kill us." His hands were braced on the truck dashboard, as he eyed the road a little harder.

I looked back at the road. "Slow. We're taking this slow," I choked out.

"Sure. We're taking it slow. You let me know the pace."

"Dating."

"Okay."

"And I'm still going out with Connor tonight." I needed to establish limits. Limits kept things slow.

"Okay." That one was more of a growl, but I wasn't going to be picky.

"Okay, then."

"Do I get to kiss you again when we part?"

OH, lord. No. Yes. No.

"Yes."

"Deal."

CHAPTER 11

I dropped Brecken off at my house and we did kiss before I left to get dressed for training and he left to work on the case. I was a little confused on which case, the insider trading or Bon's murder, but I was too focused on getting my rides done before Connor showed up to care. That was a lie. I definitely cared more about it being Bon's death.

I also was weighing Connor's date and my insistence on still going. I wasn't excited about my date after this morning and was debating if I could go through with it at all. My brain wasn't letting me move on without admitting that going out with Connor wasn't about Connor at all. I liked Brecken. Connor of the too many smiles didn't have a chance. I had barely thought of him, outside of proving that I wasn't stuck on Brecken. And I had to face that I was.

And if I was stuck on Brecken, was it fair to lead Connor on?

On the other hand, Brecken needed to see that I wasn't just waiting for him to come around and pick me up.

Which was still the wrong reason to go on a date with someone else. *Shiitake mushrooms.*

I was about to call him and cancel when Connor came up the driveway.

"Lark!" He had a huge grin on his face as he got out of his car, a folder in his hands. "How are you doing today?"

I needed to tell him I wasn't going. "Good. Connor—"

"I have the results."

Oh goodie. I knew that Tiffany already let out the good stuff, but I wanted to see if there was anything else found.

I rushed to his side, grabbing the folder and diving into the results. Most of it was in science gibberish and from what I did understand it all looked to be expected. Until I got to the toxin results. Positive for Oleander, and... nothing else. Huh. I looked further through the tests, looking for anything that would specify what tests were done. There. Negative for Banamine.

I read it again, to make sure I hadn't misunderstood before I bit my lip. Would this throw all the results off?

"Connor? This doesn't show that he was on Banamine."

"Yeah, I didn't give him any," he answered, smiling at me like he was already thinking about our date.

Come back to me, buddy.

"I did. Remember?"

His face went white, and he took the papers, looking them over.

"It must be a mistake. I'll do the tests again tomorrow. It'll be fine." His hands were jerky when he gathered all the papers back into the folder. His jaw working side to side, he rushed the folder back to his truck.

I guess I wasn't going to get to look through any more of it.

"Good catch." His smile was tight and didn't reach his eyes.

His face didn't look like he was happy I caught it. Not at all.

"I'm ready if you are. Are you sure you still want to go out tonight? Because—" I really didn't.

"Of course! I've been looking forward to tonight all day."

Why?

I mean, he wasn't as handsome as Brecken, but he smiled without it taking a court order, so I would assume he could get a date easily. Why was he out here with me looking forward to a date? Especially one in Barrow Bay.

Oh, wait. He didn't know Barrow Bay. Everyone would want to be in the middle of our date… which made me stop for a second. Why wasn't anyone here, right now? Why wasn't Lindsey trying to get the scoop on where we were going? I tried to tell myself that maybe they didn't care, but I wasn't buying. They always cared. What was I missing?

Could Brecken, mister 'no comment' himself, have told them about this morning? Or were they all waiting at The Pub? Because I was predictable. Maybe we shouldn't be predictable.

"You feel like Italian?" I asked Connor. I hated Italian, but no one would expect me to take Connor there.

Connor smiled at me and nodded.

"Perfect. Mind if I drive?" I called back over my shoulder, already heading to my truck. This date was a horrible idea, but at least I would be in control.

We both piled into my truck, Connor getting in like a normal man, which meant no holding my door open with a wicked smile.

Sigh.

I shouldn't be comparing him to Brecken, anyway. It was impossible not to, but I shouldn't. Brecken had no place on my date with someone else.

Even if I didn't want to be here anymore.

On the drive into town we chatted about people we knew in the horse business, and Connor filled me in on horse show gossip. Most of it I'd already heard from Christy, but still enjoyed hearing from his point of view. As I pulled onto Main Street, I kept an eye on the parking lot at The Pub, noticing that it was fuller than normal. Ha-ha! Called it. Then I noticed the parking lot for Andre's Italian Restaurant. Which was also fuller than normal. Huh.

"This place looks really full tonight. Must be good food."

"You would think so, wouldn't you?" I muttered under my breath. Something was up. "Maybe we should try a different restaurant?" I suggested.

"Why? This one looks good."

"Because it's never that full. It can't be good." Connor gave me a weird look. Yeah, I knew that didn't make any sense to him. He didn't know Barrow Bay. Or its people. Something was up. My Spidey sense was going off.

"I vote we still go." He was brave in his innocence.

I let out a sigh and parked in the first spot I could find. Connor jumped out of the truck with a smile, but I sat for a second more. I could do this. I could get out of this car and go on a real date with a real guy with real food. I could. Also, I really need to give up on the repetitive thing. 'Real food' was just silly.

Connor met up with me at the back of the truck and hesitated a second before turning to match my speed towards the front door.

I think he wanted to take my hand. I'm glad he caught on that we weren't there yet.

Were we?

Snickerdoodles.

I kept meaning to look up these things before this date, but I got distracted with all of Jen's drama. And mine. Or really, Tony's. This all stemmed from Tony's drama. He killed Bon. He got caught doing insider trading. He was the source of a lot of trouble.

I hoped he went down for killing Bon. I don't know how bad the jail time was for insurance fraud, but I hoped it was higher than the fines for animal abuse.

Andre's was four doors down from The Pub, but from the style and atmosphere, it should have been miles. Andre was a transplant from the East coast where the accents were thick and the swear words were plentiful. At least, that was what he was trying to get us to believe. I had heard from Gran, that when he first came here, he spoke like what we imagined people from Jersey to speak like— like any other English-speaking American. Now, after eight years of Barrow Bay antics, Andre had turned his slight verbal slip into a straight up persona that Hollywood would be proud of. Three quarters *The Godfather* and one part *The Sopranos*, eating at Andre's was like five-star dining with full TV charm. Add in all the pictures of TV mobsters on the wall, and it was everything a Californian pictured New Jersey to be: the mob-infested land of pasta and garlic.

Andre met us at the door with a wide smile. Like, really wide. My flight response had definitely kicked in, and it only got worse when his smile got wider and he turned around to yell into the dining room.

"Lark's here! Pay up!"

Oh. My. God.

"Pay up? What are they talking about?" Connor asked me.

I turned and looked at him to say… something… but I was too worried about how this could get worse to answer.

"Lark! And this must be the vet! So happy to see you. You don't even know how happy."

I'll bet. Or more to the point... *He* bet. My eyes narrowed on him and even his over the top accent couldn't make me smile.

"How much did you bet that we would eat here, Andre?" I demanded.

"Wait. They bet?" Connor asked, his brows furrowed in confusion.

Tonight was going to get worse. I knew it.

"Oh yeah," Andre told Connor. "I knew Lark hates it here, so I knew she would bring you. Everyone in the restaurant bet that you would come here in that pool. Your Gran is sitting with Helen in the corner if you want to say hi."

Oh god.

"Lark! I just knew you would come here!" Gladys jumped up from her seat with Sallie Mae and gave me a hug. "Twenty dollars and the knowledge that I know you better. Priceless!"

"Shut your gossipy mouth, you police minion! It was a good guess. You got lucky, nothing more," Sallie Mae yelled at us. I could see the whites in Connor's eye. If he had been a horse, I would be waiting for the spook.

"Well, Lark," Gladys continued, turning to Connor. "Introduce your new beau." She eyed him with a sniff. "Isn't as cute as the last one."

We could definitely say she was on Brecken's side.

"Beau?" Connor choked out.

"Beau. As in romantic interest or male admirer. Suitor. Sweetheart. Lover. Do you need more clarification?" She blinked at him, all innocence and sugar.

Lover? Oh my god. I... she... he....

I hated this town. Almost as much as I loved it.

"I think he was questioning your use of the term, not what it meant. No one really uses it anymore," I clarified for him. Gladys pinned me with a look.

"I use it. Your grandmother uses it. Are you saying we're 'no one'?"

I was out. Good luck, Connor.

"Your turn." I told Connor with an innocent smile.

Instead of glowering at me for putting him in this position like Brecken would have done, Connor went for his patented first weapon; his smile. *Good call, dude.*

It didn't work. Gladys still looked back and forth at us, waiting for something... oh. Introductions. Right.

"Gladys, this is Connor. He was Bon's vet."

"He was the vet of the horse that died?" She gave him another look up and down. Yep, definitely on team Brecken. "I would think that would be a comment on his ability to do his job."

"Gladys!" I reprimanded. "He did everything he could. Sometimes things happen."

"Especially when people poison the horse," Connor supplied.

Oh, no. I could see an angry Special Agent Asshat in my future. Wait, we were going to call him by his real name... yeah, I already forgot it. Oops.

"Poison?" Sallie Mae asked as she also got up from her table and walked over to join us. "Who poisoned who?"

"Who poisoned *whom*," I corrected under my breath. This stopped the conversation for the ladies to stare at me in confusion. "What?"

"Whom?"

For the love of… yes. I knew grammar. Well, enough, anyway.

"Just because I didn't go to college does not mean I'm stupid," I hissed at them under my breath. *Shiitake mushrooms.* I smiled at Connor, who had a college degree plus vet school, with a tight smile.

"We never thought you were, honey," Gladys said, grabbing my hands and patting them. "Just… less educated than most."

"I'm smart!" I defended myself to Connor, who was starting to look a little white. Then a lot white. What?

"Umm, why's my face on that guy's shirt?" He asked, pointing over to George, our half-blind mailman, who was sitting three tables away from us with his wife wearing a white t-shirt, the one people could buy to get a quick screen print put on it. And they did. Of Connor's face.

Fudge buckets of shiitake mushrooms.

I looked at his wife's shirt. Yep. There was Brecken's face, in all its Captain America glory. In fact, only a few people weren't wearing a white t-shirt with a face on it, and most of those people were wearing actual Captain America gear.

"How did they even pull this off?" I murmured to Gladys and Sallie Mae as I took in the room. It must have cost a fortune to get all these shirts done. And in one day.

"Well, Zach was saying that he thought you should pick Brecken because he needs to be our next Chief, and that he was going to wear his Captain America shirt to The Pub tonight to show his support. Then Ian said that a horse trainer should date a vet. That you two would be perfect for each other. So, he said that if Zach wore his shirt, he would go out and get one in support of the vet."

"Because horse trainers should date vets." Crazy. It had to be in the water.

"Yes! Then Benny heard and said that if Ian was getting shirts with your vet's face on them, then he was getting some with Brecken's. Then Lindsey posted it on the blog and ran a deal for anyone who wanted to buy one and show their support for their choice."

Lindsey. I should have known when she went silent.

"Why didn't I get the alert?"

Gladys flushed. "I may have pointed that out, so she temporarily blocked you."

It all made sense. The people needing to know who I was choosing. The gossiping in the background. I wanted to ask who the bookie was, but I was too afraid that Gladys would tell me it was Aunt Helen. Because I was pretty sure she was.

I needed coffee.

"Do you want coffee?" I asked Connor, who was eyeing the door and half-turned towards it.

"At six at night? Lark. What are you thinking?" Gladys shook her head at me.

"That I don't want to eat here anymore?" I answered gesturing to… all that.

"Good. You should go try The Pub," she suggested, her smile taking over her face.

Oh no.

"Why?" Connor asked, eyeing her with obvious reluctance. I was really impressed he hadn't run by now. Honestly, he didn't have many shirts in the crowd. It took real balls to stay in a restaurant when the town was cheering for another guy right in your face.

"Because I'm sure you two could use a drink now," Gladys gave us her best old lady smile.

I was being played. On the other hand, I was mortified here, so how much worse could it get?

"There's a place to get drinks?" Connor asked, taking another glance around the room.

I thought about suggesting the Mexican restaurant to avoid whatever was waiting at The Pub, but I had to admit that I was curious. How much worse could this get? I was on the train *and* watching it crash at the same time. Turned out, watching it crash from inside was just as fascinating as watching it from the outside. I couldn't look away. I would have thought the shirts would be the coup d'état, but Gladys's eyes gleamed like there was more. I was so weak. I had to know.

"Yep. A few, but The Pub is the best."

"You keep saying that like it's important," he commented.

"What?"

"*The* Pub."

"It's the name. It is important."

"The name is '*The* Pub'. With the '*the*'?"

I looked at him a little harder while I let him process saying 'the' twice in a row before answering. "The owner's British." I turned and walked out before he could ask what that had to do with anything. I didn't feel like explaining. "Tell Gran hi for me!" I called out to Gladys as I walked out, Connor trailing behind me.

"What just happened there?" Connor asked, still slightly dazed.

"You just got Barrow Bay-ed."

"Did you just use the town's name as a verb?"

I brought out my mock TV voice. "Do you feel dazed or confused? Have you experienced episodes of extreme confusion? Matchmaking manipulations got you afraid to talk to people? If so, you may have been Barrow Bay-ed. There's no known cure at this time, except leaving and it's known to be very contagious. You should exhibit extreme caution at all times when in the presence of all town leaders or old biddies, as they may attack at any time."

He didn't laugh.

Well... Okay.

I let my smile go dim and looked away.

I thought it was funny. Brecken would have laughed. Heck. Jen would have snorted up her drink. Connor and I were definitely not meant to be.

"Let's go," I said as I headed down the street to The Pub. Maybe if I was lucky, whatever was waiting for us would scare him off for good. I was missing Hailey, and I wouldn't mind ending this farce early to call her. He followed, still looking back at the restaurant like the town might attack. Oh, wait. I might have just told him they would. Oops. Oh, who was I kidding? The fact he might have believed me was making it really hard to keep a straight face right now.

"No, I think we need to address why people had shirts with my face and another man's on them," he insisted, his eyebrows low on his face.

"They were showing support."

"For *what?*"

Really? Was he going to make me spell this out? Fine.

"For who I should pick for dating."

"I don't know what bothers me more: that there's so much pressure on one date or that they were able to get my photo from the website and put it on a shirt."

"That's Barrow Bay for you. We do nothing small."

"No, really. Aren't those photos protected? How can they just get it and take it to a screen print place?"

I thought he was focusing on the wrong part of this equation. I would be a lot more worried that the town was voting on 'beaus' than where they got the photo, but that was just me.

"Pretty sure you can just copy it from the website. As to the shirt printer? Who knows what they did to get it done that quickly? I learned a long time ago not to ask."

"Why?"

I could hear the fear in his voice. Not sexy. Smart. But not sexy.

"You don't want to know. Trust me."

"Does the town normally bet on dates?"

Ahh, he was getting to the good stuff.

"Nope, this seems to be a special occurrence just for me. Or I should say Brecken."

"He's the other guy?"

"Yeah. The town's trying to get him to stay and be the new Chief of police and they decided I was the right lure to catch that fish."

"And did you?"

Well, there was a loaded question. One I had no intention of answering tonight.

"I'm here on a date, am I not?"

"That doesn't answer the question on if I'm up against the new Chief of Police," Connor had a grim look to his face. He wasn't happy with that thought.

"*Possible* new Chief of Police, and…" I trailed off. Honesty was the best policy, I guess. "Maybe?"

"Maybe." His voice sounded skeptical. Or he thought I, and my town, were crazy.

He might have a point there.

"You want me to drive you home?" I might as well be the bigger person.

"No. I actually am really hungry. I just don't want to stare at my own face while eating."

Good point. I could see where that would be disconcerting.

"Let's see how bad The Pub is. If it's bad, I heard a rumor that there are restaurants near the edge of town. Maybe we can find some peace there." I stopped just short of the door. "We're agreed, though, right? This—" I gestured in between us. "—isn't happening, right?"

"Wow." His face went slack, and he looked a little dazed. Oops. I guess that was too much honesty. "I have never been turned down by a girl before."

What was up with all the guys who asked me out not being turned down by girls?

"Yeah, I've heard that before." *Get to the point, dude. We're out, right?*

"Who was the last guy to say it?"

Well, this could be a little embarrassing.

"Brecken."

"The other guy? The new Chief of Police?"

"The *possible* new Chief of Police. He isn't moving currently, so it's just the town trying to manipulate people. And yes."

"Right." He squinted at me. "So, there's still a chance?"

No. "Sure. There's always a chance." Not at all.

"Then let's go find food. Then we can talk about the future."

Food sounded okay, but alcohol sounded amazing. I reached out and pulled open the door, bracing myself for whatever lay ahead.

Red. White. Blue.

EVERYWHERE.

Well, I guess The Pub had spoken.

"Is this some patriotic state holiday I don't know about?" Connor asked, taking in the decorations. Flags hung from every corner, and Joe had even painted the windows in our nation's colors. I stared at them, trying to figure out how he did that. And how I missed it from the outside.

"Nope. Just telling everyone where my loyalty lay. Thanks for the loss, by the way." Joe was trying to look angry, but I could see a glimmer of amusement in his eye.

"Please." I rolled my eyes. "You would never have put your money on your bar. You bet on Miguel's, didn't you?"

"Yep. Didn't realize you were desperate enough to go to Andre's." Joe smiled at me.

My eyes narrowed on him. He's too happy for someone that just lost a bet. "You bet on Brecken, didn't you?"

His eyes got wide, and he quickly turned away to hide his face. "Here, this way." He walked towards the back of the bar and I shook my head.

"Bet? More betting? What kind of town is this?" Connor wondered out loud as we started following Joe back, something that Joe had never done before.

It was a bar. We always seated ourselves. I didn't know if I was ready for whatever surprise awaited at the end of the escort.

"Benny! They're here!" Joe cried out, right before he stepped to the side so that I could see the table he was leading us to.

Fudge buckets of snickerdoodles.

The table that awaited us was unlike anything I had seen in there before. One, it had a tablecloth. A real, actual red, white and blue tablecloth. And candles. And… Benny?

"Benny? What are you doing here?"

"Here you guys go." Joe pushed me towards the bench, the momentum making me fall into the seat across from Benny before I could protest, then he shoved Connor into the other bench. By Benny. Who was smiling at me like a cat that just stole the cream. Well, if Connor didn't run for the hills after this, I would have to be impressed. Not enough to give him another date, but impressed, nonetheless.

"Lark! Knew you would be coming around here." Benny raised an eyebrow in challenge, and I sat there trying to figure out why he even….

Oh, for the love of….

"I'm not a bartering tool! Go away!" I snapped. Oh, wait. I could use Benny to get out of my date. Maybe I shouldn't have snapped so hard.

"Ahh, I see he told you about his lack of future plans." Benny leaned forward as if he was going to whisper something to me and I unconsciously leaned in to hear it. "He must really trust you."

Why was I leaning again? Because that wasn't worth whispering.

"Really? Because I was under the impression his old work knew about it, too. And his family. And most of the town," I said, nodding to the new decorations.

"Ahh, Lark! You are insinuating that my office leaks."

"Like a sieve."

He chuckled at me. "Still holding the leg against me, huh?"

"Wouldn't you? Lindsey posted the article before you even left the police station!"

"I can't help what someone posts on their blog."

"You could stop letting her sit next to the dispatch when the calls come in."

"I could, but then how would she get all the good gossip?"

That was the point.

"What do you want, Benny?" I asked, giving up on ever getting him to ban his goddaughter from the police station. Some things are never going to happen.

"Just to have a nice dinner with you and your new beau."

"Do you know what the word 'date' means?"

"Day on a calendar?" He shot me a triumphant smile at his cleverness, and I tried to bite back my smile.

He was right. That was funny.

"It means that we're trying to get to know each other. So, why don't I let you out so you can go about your business?" Connor interrupted, obviously taking my cheek as an excuse to get all manly about Benny leaving. That was a mistake.

"I don't believe I got your name." Benny said, eyeing him.

"Connor."

"Is that like 'Just Jack?'" Benny asked, while I held back a snort of laughter.

I couldn't wait to watch him try using that charming smile to get out of this one.

"No, more like 'just Connor,'" Connor quipped back with a satisfied smile.

Well, lookie there. We had a sense of humor. Even Benny smiled at that.

"And you are the vet of the horse that died? The one that got poisoned?"

"Yes." Connor shot me a questioning look, but I was too busy staring at Benny through narrow eyes to answer.

"Nope," I snapped. Benny looked at me, all innocent smiles and upturned hands. "No interviewing people on my date."

Connor froze, glancing from me to Benny, his mouth sagging slightly open.

"Lark, Lark. This isn't an interview. Just some friends talking."

"About a crime." I crossed my arms in front of my chest.

"Unproven crime."

"I have the test results," Connor offered Benny. "They are in my truck back at Lark's barn. You are welcome to them."

Wait, didn't we already cover that those were the wrong test results?

"No. We need to take them ourselves to maintain the chain of custody. We'll be out there to take them tomorrow."

"You're re-running the tests?" Connor's face turned white. "That's... that's not needed. I ran all the tests already."

We both turned and looked at him in surprise.

"This is an investigation for animal abuse and insurance fraud. We need to make sure everything is done correctly," Benny said, giving Connor a long look. Connor met his gaze for only a second before looking away, conceding the point.

"Connor, is there something wrong with them taking another sample?" I asked, done with all his squirrely behavior. He already knew he had to re-run them. Why would he care if the police did it for him?

"No. Nothing. They can take another sample. Saves me the effort anyway since I needed to re-run them. I just... didn't know that the police would be pulled into it so quickly."

"There was an open investigation into Tony already. Adding these charges is not difficult," Benny responded, eyeing Connor. "Lark, I'm a little vague on the details. How much Oleander is needed to kill a horse?"

"Very minute amounts," interrupted Connor.

Yep. Squirrely. He was going to start hoarding nuts any moment now.

Benny took a long look at Connor before turning to me for confirmation. Like I knew more than a vet. That was cute. I nodded a confirmation.

"Interesting," Benny murmured.

I don't think he was talking about Connor's answer, but I was mystified as to why. That was not true. I knew why Benny's police radar was going off. Connor was acting guilty as all get out. I just didn't understand why. Tony murdered the horse. Connor tried to save him.

Didn't he?

"Tell me, Connor, have you been in the area long?" Brecken asked from behind me. When I turned, I saw him approaching from the hallway where the bathrooms were.

It was official. My date had become an interview. I couldn't believe it. Next, they would be accusing Connor of killing the horse instead of Abby's husband.

"Where's your partner in paranoia?" I asked Brecken with a glare.

"Annoying Jen," Brecken replied, keeping his eyes on Connor but I still caught a slight upturn of his lips.

That was a joke. Well, Special Agent Ass Hat was probably annoying Jen, but Brecken was trying to be funny about it. My heart fluttered. Actually fluttered. That couldn't be healthy.

"Shouldn't we stop him?" I asked, concerned for my friend's wellbeing. And because I liked her out of jail.

"Nah, he seemed to be having too much fun." Brecken's smile broke all the way through this time.

Yep. Definitely a flutter. And a stomach cramp. How were these reactions indications of attraction? How did heart conditions and stomach issues equal wanting to kiss him senseless? But it did. It *so* did.

"So, you guys are going to get a court order for the horse's body, right?" Connor asked, shifting in his chair. That drew all our attention back to him.

Really? I was flirting with Brecken in front of him and he was more concerned about the horse? I was not happy. He should be jealous! Enraged! At least... care? Yes, he should at least care. He didn't, in fact he was looking at the bar.

"Yeah," Brecken said, his eyes narrowed on Connor, who met his gaze with a chin jut. Dude. He had lost the right to be arrogant when Brecken sat down next to me, and Connor was too busy talking to Benny to care.

"Well, then I'll see you Monday," Connor said, with a smirk.

Again! Why? Why was he smirking at Brecken when he was sitting next to Benny? Across the table from Brecken who was sitting by me. Didn't anyone care that we were on a date? I knew it had been a long time, but I was pretty sure that I was supposed to be the person they cared about the most.

Dating sucked.

"So, since you boys are interviewing my date and I'm still foodless, do you need me? Can one of you drive him back to my barn? I'm over tonight."

Benny checked his watch. "Seven fifteen! Who had seven fifteen?" he yelled out into the bar.

Joe stalked over, glaring at Benny before throwing the money down.

"You did. And you knew it, you cheater." Joe scowled before walking away.

"Don't be mad. I'm just better at gambling," Benny called after him.

"Isn't gambling illegal?" I asked the group.

"Not in Barrow Bay," Brecken replied.

"I'm pretty sure that state laws count everywhere. You're a policeman. You should care about this." There was no way that straight-laced Brecken bet on anything, especially a dating pool.

He shrugged. "I won."

No. NO! There was no way that straight-laced, by-the-book Brecken, gambled.

"You bet on my date?"

"And won."

"What, exactly, did you win?" I growled. Pretty convincingly, too. I would have been impressed if I wasn't too busy being angry.

"I won the girl."

Oh my. There went my heart condition again.

CHAPTER 12

Connor did end up getting a ride from Benny. After Brecken laid down his line, it was clear that I wasn't interested in Connor. He didn't seem too upset about it.

I, however, was done with the night and left everyone to go home and hide, eating my stash of M&Ms because I still hadn't gotten food.

I grabbed my phone to text Jen before I called Hailey. Might as well hang out with her since my date was a bust.

Me: *Hey, Jen. Date over. Want to come hang out?*

Jen: *When did your date end?*

She had to be kidding. Was she in on the bet? How did she not tell me about it? Traitor.

Me: *Benny won. Not hard to do when he crashed my date and started to interview him.*

Jen: *I saw. Lindsey already posted it.*

What?! How? I grabbed my phone and pulled it out. No alert. I opened the app and looked. There! There it... oh my god.

Battle of the Boyfriends

Lark Davis's big date with her new beau was tonight, and it was an unmitigated failure. After trying to go to Andre's for dinner, they weren't even seated before Lark called it and escaped to The Pub where she dumped her date on our Chief. Is this how a divorced woman acts when on a date? Dumping their men on others? I guess we'll find out when she has her next date. Hopefully she won't treat our newest potential member of the police force with similar disrespect.

Hated. I hated her. Nowhere was there any mention of the shirts! Or the decorations! Or the bets! This was not my fault! It wasn't... why was I arguing with a phone?

Jen: *You're reading it, aren't you?*

Me: *What do you think? One day she'll regret this.*

Jen: *I hope not. I love her reporting.*

Me: *Only because she's writing about me and not you.*

Jen: *True. I'll be there in five.*

Good. Maybe I could talk her into watching something Disney. I was feeling like some happy singing tonight. I headed back to my place, already dialing Hailey. A good conversation with my daughter and best friend. Tonight just took a turn for the better.

The next morning, I had to cover the rides I skipped after Bon's death, so I was at the barn early. Missy didn't work Sundays unless there was a show, so I was alone, just me, my horses, and my thoughts. And true to my habits, my thoughts went in a circle of destructive behavior. I had two options. Brecken and my corresponding emotions or overanalyzing Bon's death.

I chose death.

It was bothering me. Why was Connor acting so weird? Why did Bon get better, then die during the drive? And the most important... why hadn't I been able to get Bon to perform? Giving up on riding, I pulled out my phone and pulled up some video of him from a year ago. Massive stride, great movement. Yep, amazing. Why did he suddenly suck? Okay, so maybe 'suck' wasn't the right word. Why did he suddenly go ordinary? Nothing in the necropsy told me anything. No injury or damage had been found. Or at least none that my limited knowledge had been able to find in the results. So why the decrease? I pulled up another video, this time from more recently, and was watching it, comparing it to the first video when a car pulled up. Putting my phone aside, I used the car as an excuse to stop obsessing.

"Annie! How's my favorite cook doing?" I called out. Maybe there was soup somewhere in her car.

"Oh, Lark! Flattery will get you everywhere." Annie grinned back.

"Yes, but the important question is, will it get me pho?" I gave her my best hopeful look. I could use some pho. In my world it was liquid happiness. I couldn't hold back my squeal of excitement when she held it up. "I love you. Never leave me."

She smiled and shook her head at my excitement. "You are too easily pleased over small things."

"Please! I looked up how to make this soup. It takes like, nine hours."

"I cheat. Mine only takes five." I stopped opening the container to look at her. "Okay, no I don't. It does take nine hours, but I make a pot of the broth at the start of the week and it lasts a while."

"Well, I appreciate all your hard work," I said around a mouthful of noodles. I'm a lady like that.

"So, you want to talk about your boy troubles?"

"Oh, no. Not you, too. How much money did you lose?"

"None. I knew Brecken would win. What I wanted to know was why."

"Why would Brecken win?" Wait, was everyone in town assuming he won? Connor just… failed. That didn't mean that… fine. Whatever. He might have won.

"No, why you went on the date in the first place."

Well. Suddenly I liked my question more. There was a lot less self-reflection in praising Brecken.

"You sure we can't talk about Brecken?"

"Is he good in bed?"

Oh god.

"So… why did I go on the date with Connor…" I looked around at the barn trying to find a truth that wasn't slightly pathetic. But, then again, pathetic seemed to be my thing. "Because I needed to know if what I felt was real, or if it was just the first attractive man who showed interest."

Annie raised an eyebrow at me and shook her head. "How buried in your own world are you?"

I was not sure how to take that.

"Buried in my own world?" I questioned, trying not to be offended.

"Do you see everyone?"

Is that a trick question?

She shook her head even harder at my confusion.

"You're a pretty girl. Maybe not a movie star, but pretty. Funny. You work hard. The single men in this town would love to ask you out. You turned them all down."

"Two!! Two men asked me out. And one was a serial cheater who was sleeping with four girls at the time."

"So that makes it less real?"

Well, that was a lot of truth to be slapped with. I can see why she brought the soup. I was sure I wasn't the only one that took truth bombs better with food.

"No. I guess Brecken wasn't the first," I muttered. If it wasn't about me making sure my feelings were real, then that only left me doing it to make Brecken regret not texting me. And that was... childish. I didn't want to be that person. Especially since it didn't work. At all.

Oh, god. I was that person.

"I guess I did it to show Brecken I wasn't to be forgotten. That I wasn't waiting around for him." Yeah. That sounded good. Better than I was acting like a scorned lover getting back at her man before she took him back.

"Did it work?" she asked, her mouth lifting slightly into a smirk.

"Probably not. Last night was pretty pathetic."

"Are you sure he needed reminding?"

"Yes. You don't disappear on people you like. You text them. You call them. You make them feel wanted."

"That's quite a list. Did you make Brecken feel all those things?"

Well...*snickerdoodles.* I guess not.

"But I wasn't the one ghosting the other. I responded."

"True." She nodded at my point, seeming to agree with me.

I was instantly suspicious.

"You know, my parents raised horses," she continued.

"*Really?*" Oh. I was guessing I should have been a little less surprised at that. Asian people could raise horses. I winced. Maybe if I was going to teach Hailey to love all people equally, I might want to do a better job myself. On the other hand, I was sitting next to an admitted infamous retired drug dealer, so I was not doing too bad.

Sigh. That actually didn't really sound any better.

"Yes, Lark. Asian people can have horses, too."

"I know. Asian countries have started fielding more eventers in the international events. They are pretty good, too. Japan and China in particular have done well." Hah! I was not a complete prejudiced nincompoop. Only slightly.

She nodded, accepting my knowledge as an apology. "My father raised paints. You know… the horses with the spots." She waited for my nod before continuing. I didn't bother to point out that paints weren't the only breed with spots. Or that 'Paints' where really Quarter Horses with spots. I was guessing that wasn't relevant. "Anyway. We had six mares and one stallion. Each one was different, and I could tell who they were in a second. But then my dad bought two quarter horses, both bays. Couldn't tell the difference at all. One was broken to ride. One wasn't. You know what happened?"

Yeah, I'd seen this one before. "I'm guessing a broken arm?"

"Broken leg, but you got the point. I mistook the unbroken bay for the one that was broken to saddle."

"Didn't he freak when you put the saddle on him?" I mean, I could understand someone mistaking two horses for each other, but he should have panicked the minute she came up to him with a saddle.

"Nope. Stood there with his legs braced and ears flicking, but still let me do everything without even a protest. Dad broke him in a month. Best horse we ever had. Nothing bothered that one." She smiled at the memory. "But the point is, when you don't take the time to understand what the horse is telling you, you might miss important things."

I didn't know that the story supported that conclusion, but I was willing to follow it to her point. I wasn't listening to the horse... or in this case Brecken.

Wait.

I wasn't listening to the horse...

No...

I pulled up the video I had been looking at, and replayed the old show performance.

Could it... no... that would be impossible.

"Lark, what are you doing? I thought you hadn't found the video. Trust me, you don't want to relive that."

"I was looking at an old video of Bon.... Wait. What video?" I pinned Annie with a glare.

"Will you look at the time? I must be getting home. My sons are coming over tonight."

"Annie... What video?"

"It isn't important! Bye!" She ran out of the barn like she might catch on fire if she stayed longer. Making a mental note, I went back to my video, watching again. First video was still amazing. He was calm, relaxed and fluid. Didn't even flinch when the wind moved the judge's tent. Second video, the horse was upset and spooky. Spooked at the flowers. Spooked at the judge. It was everything Emily could do to keep him going. I thought back at the phrase that had been running through my head since day one.

It's like he's a completely different horse.

Something Abby's sister-in-law said made me pull up another video, this time of Emily on her own mount, the one that died a few months before. There was only one, taken at one of the smaller shows a year ago. A bay. With identical socks to Bon. Identical. I couldn't even tell the difference. Who was competing at one level lower than Bon. A horse that spooked twice before Emily could get him under control and to work.

Oh my god. Bon *was* a different horse.

That's why she said she had raised him. Not because she was being overly dramatic, but because she had. Could… Could Connor have been in on it, too? Was that why he was acting so squirrely at dinner last night? Why he showed up at the barn without calling? Why he always answered the phone on the first ring?

I knew that was suspicious.

Wait. This was all so crazy. And farfetched. Really far, farfetched. Tony poisoned Bon. We were all pretty sure he did it. And when the testing was done again it would show… the correct results.

Which Connor's didn't.

Oh no.

Connor had to have been in on it.

Sweet cheese and crackers. Bon had been getting better. Much better. So much better, I thought he would make it

Could he have… No. I must be paranoid. Connor wouldn't have *killed* Bon. Unless...

No. I must be paranoid. Right? Just paranoia.

Maybe I should call Brecken, just in case.

Also, I needed to find out what video was out there that I shouldn't see.

CHAPTER 13

Brecken didn't answer his phone, so I drove to Jen's house. That seemed to be the best place to find them, since the Special Agent seemed to like to annoy her. She also wasn't answering her phone, so I figured it was a good bet that she was facing down irritating FBI agents. Sure enough, when I pulled onto her street there were a few cars that weren't normally there, one of which I recognized as Brecken's.

I parked my truck and walked up to Jen's house, holding back my shudder at her house architecture. Jen and I were best friends, but sometimes it was a case of opposites attract. Where my house was all old-time cottage charm, Jen's was all fashionable beige with contemporary lines and a neat, tidy lawn. I bet her homeowners association loved her. Mine did not feel the same about me. Get a series of body parts delivered to my front door and the head of the committee had decided I was bad luck. I could see their point.

I knocked on Jen's door, ignoring her doorbell. I was too keyed up for the bell, I really wanted to feel the wood under my knuckles.

"What?" Jen demanded, getting most of the word

out before the door even opened. Her golden hair bun was drooping to the side, and she had a full glare that softened when she saw me. "Lark?"

"I need to talk to Brecken. And maybe Special Agent Ass Hat." I pushed past her, giving her a quick worried hug before walking into the living room scanning for the boys. Jen's living room was like her house, modern, beige and stylish. I hated it. It had no history. No roots.

"That's *Mr.* Special Agent Ass Hat to you, Miss Larklyn Davis." Ass Hat, himself, came out from Jen's office carrying a box of records that made her frown when she saw him.

"Ms.," I corrected absently.

"I'm sorry?"

"It's Ms. Not Miss."

"Good to know." He smirked at me, obviously one of those guys who thought mouthy women were cute.

From my experience, they only thought I was cute so long as they could out-sass me. None lasted long. Brecken followed, exiting the office with a curious glance in my direction.

"Lark, what are you doing here?" he asked, moving towards me.

"Probably making a fool of myself," I muttered.

"Just right now?" Jen joked.

I let myself glare for a second before focusing on the boys. Now that we were here, I was questioning my logic. I mean, I was definitely jumping to conclusions. Probably a few assumptions, too. Maybe I shouldn't have bothered them.

"Lark?" Brecken asked, closing the distance between us with a frown. "What's wrong?"

"I think Connor did it." Wow. What had I just thought? Didn't I just tell myself not to jump to conclusions? Instead I just blurted out the most unlikely, out of all my thoughts. They were going to think I was crazy. Scratch that. Brecken knew I was crazy. But I might have gone another level up the crazy scale.

"Lark? Do you want to tell us what you think Connor did, or do you need more time to contemplate how stupid you're feeling?" Brecken asked, using his hands to raise my face to meet his.

"How did you know I was thinking that?" I whispered. Like Special Agent A— Nic couldn't hear me clear as day.

"You wince. You always wince and then crinkle your nose. Like Samantha."

Oh, my god. He just made a Bewitched reference. I might be in love. Wait! No…

"Do not."

"Do too."

"I—"

"Yeah, no more of that. What were you saying, Lark?" Jen interrupted, still shooting daggers at Nic.

"What if Bon wasn't Bon?"

"You mean if he was Don, instead?" Nic said.

"Yes! Wait… you were making fun of me. Not nice, Special Agent A."

"A.?"

"It was pointed out that the nickname was too long. But you are earning it, so I have decided to try abbreviations."

He nodded slowly, processing this information. "And your conclusion?"

"It feels better to use the whole word. 'A.H.' is too close, and A feels too friendly."

"I kind of like S.A.A.H. Saah. It has a better flow," he replied thoughtfully.

I frowned. "It really doesn't—"

"OH MY GOD! Please stick to a topic!" Jen interrupted, glaring at the special agent.

She had a point.

"I think Emily switched out the horses." I pulled out my phone. "See, this is Bon a few months ago, before his decline."

"His decline?" Brecken asked, still a little confused.

"Wait for it. Everyone see Bon?" They all nodded. "Here's Emily's private mount from a year ago." I showed them the video. "She hadn't been showing him much, instead she focused on Bon this show season, but…"

"They look the same." Brecken murmured.

"Exactly. Only one is very talented and well-trained and the other… less." Brecken and Nic brought their gazes up to me, questioning my point. "A few months ago, Bon's performance took a big dip. Huge. Right around the same time that Emily's private horse died."

Brecken nodded. "Tiffany mentioned that. Mentioned that Emily was struggling mentally."

"Yes! So Emily's horse dies, and Bon suddenly stops performing at the same level. We all thought it was a slump. It happens." Boy, did it happen. If I had a dollar for every time a horse suddenly forgot how to turn, I would have my own Olympic horse. "Especially if the rider is having a hard time. But when they switched him to me, he didn't improve. I was thinking the horse had something wrong with him."

"Because he wasn't performing?"

"Exactly. And that's not all. Abby didn't tell Emily when she was taking the horse. Emily followed the trailer to tell me that I couldn't take her horse. The horse she, and I quote, 'raised.' I thought it was just her being melodramatic at the time, but…"

"Now you think it might be literal," Brecken nodded as he wrote something down in his little book.

One of these days I was going to grab that book and see what it actually said. I wondered if everything in it even had to do with cases.

"Yeah. I mean, it's all circumstantial, but…"

"It's pretty telling." Brecken frowned at his notebook before he looked back at me. "But why? And what does Connor have to do with it?"

"A gut feeling?" I gave him a sheepish look. "He showed up at my barn without notice. He always answers my phone calls." Yeah, that didn't sound crazy, at all. "Frankly, I have never had a vet do that. Most of mine are too busy. They just call me back after they finish with whatever horse they were with. And the test results? The ones from the necropsy… that he *insisted* he do himself.

Son of a biscuit." I felt like hitting something. He had to be involved. "They were wrong. The test results, that is. I called him on it, that they didn't have the right results, before we went on the date. He promised me that he would look into it."

"I have to admit, with his behavior that makes more sense," Brecken told Nic. "He was really squirrely. Looked like he was trying to hide something. Benny and I just assumed it was a girl back home." Brecken shot me a guilty look that I waved away.

"He was very interested about you needing a warrant for the body, right?" I was starting to have some concerning thoughts.

"Yeah, he was weird about that, too."

"What if that's because he's going to try to destroy the evidence?"

"So, the cause of death might have been falsified. *And* you have another suspect," Nic summarized. Brecken seemed to catch on to his hint and glowered at him.

"I get it. Not your problem anymore. Whatever. Stay here terrorizing innocent townspeople," Brecken muttered at him.

Nic just smiled back, hefting his box up while Jen sent him angry looks from the corner.

"I'm going to go call this in." Brecken turned and walked outside, already dialing his phone.

"I hate you," she hissed. "A normal cop would go off and finish the case. Catch the bad guy. You're a freak!"

Wow. "Umm, Jen? Don't we normally like to be nice to the police officers? Especially when they're investigating... well... you?"

"He isn't a police officer. He's a child of Satan." Jen gestured at him like he was going to sprout horns and a pitchfork any second.

I waited. I admit, I was disappointed nothing happened.

Also... Maybe Jen should come with us. And away from the man that could put her in jail.

"I assure you, my parents are very nice people. My evil is completely self-taught," Nic smiled at Jen. Then again, he looked like he was enjoying it.

"You must be such a disappointment to them," she fired back.

I was kind of proud. He really brought out the fire in her.

"Oh no. They worship me. I'm their baby boy."

"Well, I could see that. You certainly are a baby," she threw back at him.

Yep. Jen needed a cooldown. I snagged her and threw her house keys at Nic, who caught them with one hand while balancing the box in the other. Impressive.

"Come on. We're leaving," I told her.

"I can't leave him in my house, unsupervised!" Jen protested. "He could... he could... get into files he shouldn't."

"Brecken? Can you find someone to keep him to just his files?" I called out to Brecken who was coming back up the walkway.

"We have a warrant for the whole house. And office. Sorry, Jen. He can look at everything."

"Ass hat!" she yelled at the house. "Stay away from my stuff!"

"I promise I won't tell anyone about the sex toys in your nightstand," came the response from inside. Jen turned another shade of red and I grabbed her arm, forcing her into Brecken's car before she could say anything else.

"Quick! Lock the doors!" I hissed at him.

"Lark, this is a mostly normal car. It doesn't—"

"Lock the back doors, or I swear to God you'll regret it."

He took out his keys and hit the lock button. "Locked. And you are scary, you know that, right?"

"I ride a 1200-pound mare that bites people when they get too close. Yes. I'm aware I'm scary." Not that Twice, my daughter's ill-named monster of a mare, believed it. I was convinced that mare would take on a tank if it came into the barn and bothered her. But it sounded good.

"I don't know what you are talking about. Twice is a sweetie," Brecken smirked. Yeah, he knew the mare adored him. Smug brat.

"Jen's going with us," I told him, changing the topic.

"Umm… No. Because I'm going to the vet hospital. So Jen's going with you."

"*Umm… Yes.* Because we're going to the vet hospital. With you."

"No. You're both staying here."

"Do you even know what colic is?"

He glared and crossed his arms.

"Or what results should show on the test?"

Thud. Thud.

We both turned to look at Jen banging on the window. I could see her yelling what I was pretty sure was 'let me out,' but I couldn't hear a thing. Brecken's car was impressively sound proof. Good to know. Not that I would… thirty-year olds didn't… back on topic.

"I'll figure it out," Brecken muttered, turning back to me.

"Or have the contacts to get the blood today? If you can get the lab tech there, of course."

"We need a warrant." He folded his arms, but his slightly pursed lips told me he was listening.

"Not if the owner consents, right?" Come on… take the bait.

"You think you can get Abby to consent today?" His arms unfolded and he started rubbing his forehead. We were in.

"I think I can get Abby there to sign the consent form in an hour." I was winning, I could see his face softening. "At most." Come on, Brecken.

Finally, he sighed. "Call her. If she can be there in an hour, you can come."

Yes! I did a little happy dance that made Brecken roll his eyes as he walked over to the car. Then he stopped, gesturing for me to call.

I dialed. "Abby?"

"Lark? Why are you... Oh. Bon's stuff. I... um..."

"I don't think your husband killed Bon." Silence.

"I'm sorry? You want to run that past me again?" She sounded a mixture of confused and angry.

Social skills. At some point I needed to get some.

"I think that someone else killed Bon and we need to take a blood test to confirm."

"I'm confused." She paused, and I let her think about everything I just blurted out. "Who do you think killed Bon?"

"Connor. I think Connor did it. I'll explain more later."

"You're a trainer, right? *Just* a horse trainer?"

That sounded mean. "Yes, but he was killed in my barn. Potentially, right in front of me. Honestly? I'm pissed."

"So you are running around playing detective?"

Ouch. That sounded stupid when she put it that way. "Pretty much."

"And the detectives are allowing this?"

"I blackmailed him. Said I could get you to release his blood to us without waiting for a warrant."

"Well, okay then." She paused again to think. "Okay, see you at the hospital." We both hung up, and I turned to face Brecken.

"See! Even Abby thinks this is a bad idea." He had his arms crossed again, leaning against the car.

"But she's coming." I walked towards him so that we were both standing, facing each other.

"Bad idea."

"I got her. Get in the car and drive." I gestured to the car, which brought both of our attentions to the angry woman in the back seat.

"One problem." He pointed at Jen who was still banging on the window.

"Hmm, I thought she would have figured out she could open the car door from the inside by now. Do you think we could get in before she got out?"

His 'you've got to be kidding me' look was epic. And correct. I walked back to look Jen in the eye. Jen mouthed 'let me out, or else'. There may have been some swear words. And a middle finger.

"Jen, you're going with us. Stop trying to escape. If you come, I'll see if we can prank Nic when we get back." I made sure every word was clearly accented so she would understand.

Jen sat back, folding her arms and narrowing her eyes at me. I crossed my heart, and she nodded. Then glared some more.

"We can get in." I told Brecken, who hesitated.

"You know you shouldn't prank an FBI agent, right?"

"He mentioned her sex toys. It's on."

He looked pained but nodded.

"I know nothing."

"Noted."

CHAPTER 14

The drive to the vet hospital was slow. Probably, because the only conversation was about how much Jen hated Nic. And how he was being a jerk. And about how he didn't need to be mean. There was something about a black heart that she refused to explain, as well as a few complaints about him and tea. Basically, she hated him. Rinse and repeat. I stopped trying to be supportive after the third round. In fact, after the second round, I wasn't sure if she really needed us, or if she was trying to convince herself. I did, however, fire off a text to Gran, asking her to pick up Hailey in case Blake was there before I made it back.

Brecken looked mildly green.

"Brecken! You're a man. Why—" Jen turned to face him before he cut her off.

"Nope." Brecken just kept his eyes on the road, refusing to acknowledge Jen.

"'Nope'? You can't say—"

"Nope. I'm not getting involved."

"You're the local contact."

"Not in this. Personal relationships with members on the team do not fall under the purview of the case."

189

I snickered.

"But… but… you still have a penis."

He glared in the mirror at her. "I said no. I'm not getting in the middle of whatever this is."

"So, you agree with me. He isn't acting professional. Professionals don't—" She stopped. "They don't act like him!"

"Still not getting pulled in."

She sat back, crossing her arms and pouting. "Where are we going, again?"

"Seriously?" I turned around to look at her. "How could you have missed the whole point of this drive? Dead horse? Vet who may be destroying records? Horse switch? Any of this ring any bells?"

"Okay, yeah, I remember some of that. Why are we going?"

"I needed to coordinate with the police team at the hospital," Brecken replied.

"What?" He had called in a team? But we…

"The team I called in because we're not securing the body of a dead horse, from a possibly deadly vet, by ourselves. One, the drive would take too long. Two, because calling in the local cops makes them happy, and three, because Jen and you are civilians and you have a daughter to think about."

Well played, Brecken. Well played.

"Fine." I checked my phone, texting Abby that the police were already at the hospital. She texted back that she knew. Paperwork was signed. She had been sent home. That made sense since her home in San Francisco was much closer to the vet hospital than I was.

I was feeling rather useless now. The local cops would do all the exciting parts. Plus, killing a horse wasn't even a crime that got serious attention. The sad truth was that the only reason the cops were there was because of Tony's investigation and the possible insurance fraud.

"Why are we going?" I asked, defeated.

"You and Jen, because you blackmailed me, thinking it would be exciting. Me, because I need to make sure they know the details of the case and to hand over the notes for the animal cruelty charge," Brecken shot me a gloating smile.

Yeah, he won. He was also a horrible winner.

"So, we're just handing over the notes?"

"Yep. They'll be taking over the case. Since Tony isn't involved, we have no jurisdiction."

"Great. So glad we took the car ride with you," I muttered.

"Yeah, other than Jen complaining in the background, it turned out pretty well for me. I would have had to drive by myself."

We were pulling in and he was right. There were several police cars and a large van that I assumed was the crime scene team.

"Can you guys wait here? This should only take a few minutes." Brecken got out of the car and walked over to meet with a few of the cops, leaving the car running.

"So, do you think I could keep the business going?"

"Business?" What was Jen talking about?

"My business. If Nic leaves me anything."

"Do you really dislike him, or are you mad at your partner and taking it out on Nic?"

Jen snorted. "You're not supposed to ask that question." She shifted and looked away from me for a second. "I'm angry at all of it. I worked so hard, and there's a good chance that he threw it all away for a quick buck."

Well, the 'he' in that statement could only mean her partner, Henry, so I guess Nic was getting the brunt of some emotional baggage that he might not be totally worthy of.

"Is it done? Your business, I mean?"

"I don't know. I mean, Henry was going to retire, anyway. Sell me his portion of the company outright. I could just give his customers to someone else and keep my existing customers. Maybe hire a new CPA to train? What do you think?" She blinked up at me, hope in her eyes.

"Do you want to do that?" It sounded good. Like something a good friend would say. Plus, I had doubts about how happy her job really made her. She had a lot of options. Maybe this was a sign she should look into them.

"Yes!" She looked away. "No. Maybe?" Her shoulders slumped, and she stared out the car window. "It gives me security. I like security."

"It gave you the FBI. I think you should return your security and ask for your money back."

She snorted out a laugh. "At least he was a hot FBI agent."

"I think any FBI agents are a sign for a new job."

"But I own the business. It's not like I can just quit. There are people working for us."

"Who?" Because she had never mentioned them.

"I don't know, but Henry has people."

"Do you think your clients will stay?" I mean, I still didn't really get what insider trading was, but it sounded bad. And Martha Stewart went to jail for it. That means it's bad.

"Most. I think. Pretty sure. I mean, if they are willing to trust me still, I'm obligated to stay, right?"

"No. I don't think you're obligated to stay, even then."

"No, if they stay, I should keep the business open."

Hmm, I don't think my opinion was being heard. Time for blind support. "I'm sure most will stay, Jen. You'll be fine. You're a wonderful CPA."

"You only say that because I do your taxes for free."

"And you drink with me."

"Yep. Those are definitely the signs of a great CPA," Jen said sarcastically from the back seat.

"But they are my favorite skills." That got me a snort of laughter from her.

"Do you think I did the right thing?" Jen's voice had gone soft again.

"Right thing? What did you do?" I really needed to look up what insider trading was.

"I sent in the tip on Tony. This is all my fault. Maybe I was just overreacting."

"They froze his assets. I don't think you were overreacting," I pointed out. Hold up. That was a good point. "If his assets were frozen, why would he have tried to kill Bon right now?"

"The insurance payout wouldn't be in the frozen accounts. It was kind of impressive had he realized that loophole. Horrible, but impressive. They also haven't officially charged him yet."

"Does that mean he's innocent?"

"No. Just that they are not ready to charge him," she admitted.

"Well, then, you're just waiting now." I didn't really know what to say to help.

"Pretty much." Jen fell silent, contemplating everything that had happened.

I scanned the group of police hanging around the front door to find Brecken. He had stopped on the outskirts of the parking lot, a little further out from the black and white cop cars. Now that it was silent in the car, I was starting to notice little things.

Like that the forest completely surrounded the parking lot.

And it was getting dark.

We should stop for dinner on the way back. Maybe—was that movement in the forest?

Was someone out there?

By the time my head turned, I didn't see anything.

"Jen? Did you see anything?"

"No." She was still obsessing over her own issues.

I must be getting a little paranoid. It was probably nothing. I was just jumpy after my last interaction with crime.

I was doing what I had been told. I was perfectly safe inside a cop's car. Being a good girl.

Suddenly the driver side door was opened, and a man in a black mask was sliding into the driver's seat. "Shit! Why are the two of you in here? Too late now, we're going for a drive."

Hold up. I knew that voice.

"Connor?" Also, couldn't he see us when he walked up? Maybe he was creeping while bending over to not be seen by the cops and didn't look in the windows. Bad planning.

He was dressed in black from head to tail. He even had the ski mask.

"Shit. Lark? What the hell?" He turned to look at me before glancing back. "Of all the freaking cars, you two had to be in this one?"

"There were a lot of cars!" I pointed out.

Wait. I don't want to be arguing with him. I turned to open the door.

It locked.

I unlocked it.

He locked it.

I unlocked it.

He locked it.

"STOP!" I turned around and glared. "Let us out." He could have the car. I wasn't insane.

"Nope. But if you stop trying to escape, I won't kill you."

"With what? Your—"

He lifted his left hand, which had a gun in it, as his right shifted gear into reverse.

"Do I want to know why you went silent?" Jen asked from the back seat.

"Nope."

"Great." She fell silent for a second. "I hate you."

"I hate me, too," I agreed. This was the last time I pushed myself into an investigation.

Hmm, I was sure I promised myself that during the whole body-part investigation, too. Maybe this time I would learn my lesson. Probably not.

"Yes. Now shut up. I need to think," Connor yelled. He was using the hand with the gun to drive, like I did when I was eating.

That wasn't a safe idea. I didn't know much about guns, but I did remember that they were sensitive. Or maybe their triggers are sensitive? Was the trigger different than the gun itself?

Connor pulled out, wheels spinning as he cut off two cars coming out of the driveway and onto the street. I was too busy grabbing the door handle to look behind us, but I was pretty sure that the two cars he cut off had crashed into each other trying to avoid us. I didn't know what was worse, his driving or the gun.

"So, what's the plan here?" I was pretty sure police cars have GPS. Would this one? Or my... oh my god.

WHY do I keep forgetting I have a phone? Pulling it out I pressed dial again.

Anyone else having flashbacks? I'd known Brecken for only a few weeks and the minute he showed up I was facing a gun. Again.

My call went through to John. He didn't talk last time I made a lifesaving phone call. I trusted John.

"Shut up!" Connor yelled again.

Well, okay then. No evil monologue. I bit my lower lip. Being disappointed was the wrong reaction, right? I mean, evil monologues were boring. The bad guys just told the hero their whole plan and then threatened them a little before the hero finds a way to escape. I wish I could say it was the escape part that appealed to me, but I was having a nasty need to know *why*.

He had a gun.

I tapped my finger as we got on the road heading back out to the freeway.

He also had my why: *why* did he kill a horse in my care?

Gun. Death. Hailey living with her father for the rest of her life.

"Why? Can I just know why?" *Shiitake fudge balls.* This was a personality trait I needed to have professionally dealt with as soon as I was out of this situation.

"Lark!" Jen hissed from the back. "Stop annoying the man holding a weapon."

"I have to know. I have issues!" I hissed back.

"You are really weird, you know that?" Connor groaned.

"Yes," Jen interrupted. "I've told her."

"Why are you two here?" Connor demanded, flashing an angry look at both of us. Well, at me and then into the rearview mirror, assumedly at Jen.

"In the car or—" I asked.

"In the car." Another glare.

"Because I thought I would be useful to the detectives. I wanted to know why Bon died." I sighed. It really was a stupid explanation now that I said it out loud.

"Oleander," he snapped.

"Really? You just kidnapped two people. I think we can drop the Oleander excuse."

"I didn't kidnap you." He was defensive.

"Okay. Good, because if you didn't, I would like out. That corner will do. You can take the car." I thought it was a good deal.

"You know who I am," he snapped.

"I have a bad memory. So does Jen. We've already forgotten everything."

"I can't believe this was the only car that wasn't a police cruiser," he muttered.

"There was the van." I had no control over my mouth. None. Because if I did, it would have stopped talking as soon as the bad man got in the car.

"I couldn't escape in the van! It had crime… scene stuff in it."

Crime scene stuff? That was the best a veterinarian with eight years of advanced schooling could come up with?

"Why didn't you have your own car?" Jen asked from the back.

Okay. That *was* a better question.

"I did. They already found it." He turned right, onto the freeway. Going... West?

"Why are we going west?" Because there wasn't a whole heck of a lot out west of here. Just a few towns that barely qualified and... forest. *Snickerdoodles.* Forest sounded bad.

"Shut. UP."

That was a good idea. Not angering the man with the gun was a good idea.

Could I look at my phone without the screen lighting up and alerting him I had it? Probably not.

I started tapping the door armrest. I was trapped and the driver was waving around a gun.

I could count all the ways my brain thought of for me to try for the gun, most of them ending in my death...

I needed to stop.

"Stop tapping!"

"I'm sorry! You're not monologuing, and I have questions, and it had to come out in some way."

That got me a long glance from Connor. Too long. "Road! Focus on the road!" I squealed as the car started to drift in my direction.

"Monologuing?"

"A prolonged talk or discourse by a single speaker. In this context, generally outlying their evil plan of world domination." I told him. See? I listened in high school.

"Only the first part of that definition is correct. The second part comes from too many superhero movies," Jen interrupted, her voice indicating that she was probably rolling her eyes.

I gasped and spun around. "You take that back. I'm brand loyal! Marvel to the end, baby. I'm a one-franchise girl."

"Hey, one-franchise girl, you know that the man driving has a gun, and he wants us to stop talking, right?" Jen reminded me.

"You were the one who brought up superheroes," I muttered as I turned back around.

"Will you two SHUT UP?!" Connor snapped at us. "I'm trying to think."

Hmm, it was concerning that he had to think so hard. Then again, he just committed double kidnapping and grand theft auto of a vehicle. I didn't have any brilliant ideas on how he could get out of this alive and free, either. And since his planning ability was directly tied to my ability to get out of this car without being shot, I would've completely given him a plan if I had one.

I took the risk and glanced at my phone. John was listening. I needed to get him our location.

"So, are we going to just keep driving towards the beach?" I asked quietly.

"Shut up."

"You talked more when we were on our date."

"Shut UP! I only went on the date because Emily wanted to know how much you knew."

"So, you're saying I was a sympathy date. Ouch. That stings." I kept the sarcasm strong in my voice. Even though it did sting. More than a little. "I'm pretty, and funny, and a great catch, I'll have you know."

"You are crazy. Your town is crazy. You're even crazier for living there!"

"That was just mean," I said under my breath. "When did you guys switch the horses?"

"What?!" He looked over at me again, this time instead of anger, his eyes were wild and panicked.

Not good.

"How did you know we switched them?"

"Watched too many videos of Emily while trying to figure out why I failed to ride Bon well. I'm assuming that the real Bon died?"

"Coliced," Connor admitted, his shoulders slumping. "Twisted a gut. Emily and I were… distracted and didn't notice."

I could guess what they were distracted doing.

"So, Emily decided to switch the two horses? So that Abby would keep paying her for training and shows?"

"Emily thought the only reason that her horse was behind was the lack of attention. She was always focused on Bon. She said if she just had the time, she could make him into a star."

Stupid. One, I rode him. He was not built to be a Bon. No amount of love and wishes were going to make him world-class. He could have gone Grand Prix level, though. He had been talented. Two, if you have two talented horses in your barn, you put the time and energy into both. Not one over the other. Stupid mistake. Your personal horses were your selling tools. Other industries have websites and brochures, we had our personal horses. They were the example of what we could do when hired.

Bob was a retired Grand Prix horse, the one I got my medals on and the one that Missy was getting hers on. Decorated school master who could pack around a kid or trainer. Twice had the talent to be close to world class if I could convince her to follow my lead long enough, but I wasn't counting on it. Greg, my third horse and current show mount, was at the second highest level. Again, not world class, but I was confident we would be able to make it to Grand Prix, the highest level, and place well in local competitions.

All were high performing, talented animals that were always groomed and maintained. I may not be great at advertising, but I knew where the most effective examples of what I could do were, and I made sure that they were ready at all times.

"Then Abby pulled him out of Emily's barn and put him in yours." He shot me a look of disgust, his upper lip curling back. "We thought it would be fine, but you started asking questions. 'Did we check him for injuries? Could there be pain?'" He raised his voice to mock mine. "We knew it was only a matter of time before you took the horse in for a full checkup. And that the x-rays wouldn't match. Not to mention we never got the new chip registered in his name. The hacker was a hack."

Wow. I might have gotten the horse killed just doing my job. "Why didn't you just own up that it was the wrong horse?"

He sent me a look that told me he didn't have a high opinion of my brains. Hey, I wasn't the one that kidnapped people to escape the cops. I firmly believed I was smarter than he was. He took an exit onto a smaller street, but I missed the exit sign while I was listening to him talk. I think it was time to accept that there will be no spy or cop job in my future. I get distracted way too easily. And I make bad decisions. Very, very bad decisions.

I was going to work on those bad decisions.

"Emily had defrauded Abby of thousands of dollars, not to mention the insurance pay out. It would have been better for everyone if the horse just died of the poisoning. So, when he coliced, I put him down. Abby would have bought a new horse. You would be blamed. Everyone was happy."

Except me. I would not be happy.

"But no. You even messed that up. Spotting the issues in the necropsy. Pointing them out to the cops. Finding the Oleander. You. Everything comes back to you."

"Anyone else feel like there should have been something about meddling kids and getting away with it in that story?" Jen muttered from the background.

"We missed dinner. A Scooby snack would not be amiss right now," I answered her.

"Oooh. Those little graham cracker ones in the shape of a dog bone?" Jen's head popped into my peripheral. I guess I wasn't the only one hungry. Interesting that fear only overrode half of my hunger and general obsessiveness. Jen also seemed to be handling the stress with sarcasm and bluffing. I was starting to think there may be a reason we were friends.

Or it might be because both of us worked in a high-stress job where we had to handle stressful and potentially terrifying situations with calm and logic.

Oh my god. I wondered if there was a way to put that as an advertising slogan. *I keep my cool, through guns and shows...* No. That doesn't work. I'd have to get back to it at another time.

"Are we on our way to Misne?" Jen asked from the back.

I looked around. Hey! She was right. And now John knew where we were. Go Jen.

"I need to think."

He needed to think, so he was driving us home?

Wait, could I think for him? Like, say, if he dropped us off, he could... head towards the border? The Mexican border maybe? It was only like an eight- or nine-hour drive. And it was dark. That would help with the cover. He just needed to get rid of us first.

Maybe I wouldn't say that last part. Getting rid of us could take on some very sinister meanings, and I had a daughter to get back to.

"So... about that plan..." I started, thinking I might throw the Mexico plan out there, just in case.

"Stop talking or else I will—" He cut himself off, or at least lowered his voice to under what we could hear. I could see his mouth still working like he was talking to himself.

Plan. I watched the scenery for a second, watching as the forest receded into a big field.

A hay field with a large hay roll near the road. I had a bad plan.

"Jen?" I looked back. "You're seat-belted, right?"

"Yes? Lark...." I could see her reach up and grab the handle on the top of her door.

I watched the roll. Five... four... three... two... one. NOW.

I grabbed the wheel and turned it to the right as much as I could. Connor slammed on his breaks and we skidded. I let go, our direction set and grabbed the handle and held on, praying not to hear the crash.

Please hit.

Please hit.

I would never investigate another crime again.

Really, this time.

Please hit. And let us survive.

CHAPTER 15

Knock, Knock.

I opened my eyes slowly, turning towards my left at the sound, and there was John, his gun out and pointed at Connor. I looked to my side window, seeing Zach, one of our other policemen, in nearly the same position. The Cavalry was here.

And my head hurt. A lot. I think I preferred punching to crashing as life-saving defensive methods.

"So... can we get out now?" I whispered, my hands instinctively raising. I knew I was the victim, and that they weren't aiming at me, but still. They had guns. My hands went up.

"Maybe?" Jen answered. I glanced back. Her hands were up, too. "How long were we out?"

Hah! I was not the only one with see-guns-put-hands-up reflexes. "I don't know."

Slowly, Zach reached out with one hand, the other still pointing the gun at Connor, opening my door. Or tried to, since it was locked. His face when it didn't open would be funny. Later. When I was less scared, tired, and hungry.

"Can I unlock it?" I yelled through the door. I probably just could have done it, but I wasn't going to do anything stupid around a man with a gun pointed near me.

Well, stupider than I had already. Good news was that Zach knew my mouth had an issue with speaking before thinking when I was stressed. Everyone in town knew, thanks to Lindsey.

Zach nodded, and I reached over to unlock the door before he pulled it open, trying to pull me out around the deployed airbags.

"Seatbelt!" I yelped as I rushed to get it unbuckled.

"You know, you really suck at being rescued," Zach muttered as he pulled me behind him.

"Yeah, I think I realized that about the time I was raising my hands thinking, 'don't shoot.'"

"Yeah, why did you do that? You were the victim. We weren't aiming at you." Zach sent me a look before focusing on Connor, who John had pulled out of the car and was handcuffing.

"There was a gun pointed at me. I figured better safe than sorry," I muttered, picking at some hay that had fallen into the car. "Where's Brecken?"

"He and the other cops got hung up in traffic. Connor caused an accident and they got stuck behind it. We were all tracking Brecken's car, so we got here first."

Jen got out of the back and joined me, walking funny, one hand rubbing a bruise on her forehead.

"Are you hurt? Why are you walking like that?" I whispered to her.

"Why do you think?" She hissed back.

I just lightly shook my head. I didn't know. "No, seriously, are you injured?"

"I have to pee." Her voice took on a slightly feral edge.

I was guessing this was a rather eminent concern. One that she was going to do anything to avoid mentioning to…

"So, I stay behind, and you get kidnapped? Was that a scream for my attention?" Nic came sauntering over, drinking something from a hot cup. When he got close enough, I got a whiff. Vanilla and cinnamon. Huh. I knew that smell. That's Jen's favorite tea. The one she got from my Gran's tea house. Interesting. I wonder if he made some of her tea on purpose. Also, she was going to kill him when she found out he took some of her precious tea. Hmm, I had better start coming up with places to hide his body.

"I did not get kidnapped!" Jen yelled at him.

I cleared my throat a little. I think the bladder pressure had gotten to her.

"Okay, I might have gotten kidnapped a little. But it was your fault! Had you not been at my house, I wouldn't have gone."

I snorted at that one. Please. Jen would have been right beside me wanting to know every detail of what was going down. I was not the only nosy one in this friendship.

Oh. My. God. We were nosy.

We were the next generation of sewing circle biddies. It was us! We were already nosy and had an irresistible need to be in the center of drama. Hence, me butting my nose into this case and the last one. We were my Gran. Well, the next generation.

I needed a drink.

"Did you just snort at me?" Jen swung towards me with fire in her eyes.

Oh, no. The pee pressure had gotten to her. She had gone off the deep end. Time to intercede.

"I need to pee. Is there a bathroom around here?" See? Look at all that self-sacrifice right there. I was a good friend.

She still glared.

Okay, so maybe I shouldn't have snorted at that. Oops.

"You're going to have to hold it," Nic said, casting a smirk at Jen like he knew I was lying to cover for her.

Though… now that we were talking about it, and the adrenaline was going down, a potty break sounded good.

"And if I can't?" I asked, casting a cautious glance at Jen. No. I really didn't think she could wait. Her eyes said, 'now or else.'

He shrugged and pointed to the side of the road. "Bushes." The hay roll was covered in cops. Not an option.

Jen and I both stared at the bushes. All three had short green stems with very little leaves. Not a lot of undergrowth in this area of the forest. Or the field. "You could hide behind a tree." I pointed out, trying to be supportive even though peeing without any toilet paper was awful and unhygienic.

"I can hold it," she snapped.

I arched my eyebrows at her. She was standing slightly on one hip, awkwardly holding her legs together.

"I can!" She glared at both of us threateningly.

"You know peeing in a cop car is going to be more embarrassing, right?" I whispered under my breath, hoping only she would hear me.

She sighed, her shoulders drooping before she turned and walked off. "I hate you!" she yelled back as she stomped towards a cluster of three trees with one bush underneath. A short bush. Very short bush. Unfortunate.

"Wide stance, Jen. Trust me. Wide. Stance."

She didn't seem to appreciate my advice from the middle finger she gave me as she walked away.

"She seems extra feisty today." Nic came up beside me, watching Jen walk away. More specifically, watching the sway of her hips. Guess the attraction wasn't one-sided.

I also noticed John watching Nic with a thoughtful look. Nic's appreciation had not gone under the radar. I gave it four months before he was back for some excuse or another. Then maybe Jen would be more sympathetic when I complained about the town and their manipulations.

"She gets that way when people come after her," I said, pinning him with a warning look and folding my arms. Time to get some answers. If he was going to be a real potential town addition, I needed to make sure that he was up to my standards for my best friend.

"We aren't after her," Nic snapped. "She's just… protective of people she shouldn't be."

Hmm. He was right about that. That meant he'd been paying attention.

"Jen's a good person."

"We know," he said softly. "We just have to catch all the people involved. I have to do my job or people could get hurt."

"Jen could get hurt," I pointed out. Jen was putting up a good face, but I knew that she was hurting from her partner's betrayal.

He winced at that but nodded. "She might be disappointed in people. She might be hurt that people aren't really who she thought they were. But Jen's strong. She called an FBI agent 'Satan' because he was doing his job when she didn't think the warrant should cover all the business records. She's protective, strong and one hell of an accountant. She'll survive this."

Yep. Smitten. I watched John smile from across the car. Huh. I guess he could hear us. Nic just clinched his future and didn't even know it.

"Welcome to Barrow Bay," I told him, walking towards a cop car. I didn't really care which one. I just needed to get one on the road so that I didn't have to copy Jen. I had peed in enough bushes in my time. Show life is not always glamorous.

"What do you mean? I've been here for days," Nic called out after me.

"That wasn't what I meant. Have fun figuring it out," I called back.

***

Zach had a jacket and a granola bar waiting for me when I got over to him.

"Brecken is almost here. They got the accident cleared, but it cost them time. He should be here in a moment."

"Good. Can he take me home?"

"We need to interview you as to what happened."

"Can't Jen do that?" Yep. My voice hit whiny. That was definitely a whiny note. Plus, I didn't know that I wanted to be here when Brecken got here. He was going to yell. He hadn't wanted me to go. Kept reminding me that cop business was dangerous. I ignored him and got kidnapped. He was never going to let me live this down.

"Lark!" An angry voice echoed in the trees as Brecken searched for me.

Yep. I didn't want to be here. "I'll make sure Gran never suggests another tea to you ever again if you take me back to Barrow Bay now. Right now. As in before Brecken gets here." I didn't get down on my knees yet, but I was thinking about it. A potty and no Brecken was motivation enough for me to be willing to beg.

"I kind of like her teas now. They did help," Zach said with an evil smile.

Liar.

"Lark! Where are you?" Brecken's voice came through the crowd, which parted so I could see him coming. The minute he saw me, his lecture started. "I told you not to come! I told you! But you just had to do it. Had to be there when we collected the evidence."

"I stayed—"

"I don't care where you stayed! You got kidnapped!"

Well. That was a fine attitude. "I stayed in the car with Jen. Who would've thought Connor would be there?" Oops.

"You did! That was why we went there tonight. Because we thought Connor was going to destroy evidence."

"And I would have, if Lark hadn't been such a nosy bi—" Connor stopped talking as John pushed him, cutting him off.

"You have the right to remain silent. Please use it." John used the momentum to throw him into the back of a Barrow Bay cop car.

"He really has the Scooby-Doo villain thing going. How did you go out on a date with him?" Jen asked as she came up beside me.

Guess she was done. I eyed her hands, which she had placed in her pockets. Eww. Definitely didn't get to wash them. I needed to get this conversation on the road before I joined her.

"He had a nice smile, and Brecken was taking me for granted," I responded.

"I was not taking you for granted," Brecken practically yelled. Everyone was now watching, although most were pretending not to stare openly.

Time to go on the offensive. "Are you going to take me to a bathroom?" I demanded.

"A bathroom?" He recoiled slightly, trying to figure out where the bathroom comment came from.

"Yes. A bathroom. You want to prove that you don't take me for granted? Well I need a bathroom. Like, in five minutes. Figure it out."

"You just made me pee behind a tree!" Jen protested.

"I didn't have to go as bad. I have time to make someone cater to me." I flashed her a sympathetic look before Brecken grabbed my arm and dragged me to the car he came in.

Or, at least I assume it was the car he came in, as he shoved me into the passenger side with a quick, "Stay," before getting into the driver's side.

He was silent as he drove towards Barrow Bay, and I bit my lip nervously. I had done something a little reckless. He was right that he told me it was a bad idea and I blackmailed him into it, but I was also right that he would never let me do something that he truly thought was dangerous.

"I did stay in the car. I followed your instructions." That thought kept running through my mind. I had been good, why had I been rewarded with a kidnapping?

"Murder cases are dangerous!" His words exploded from him and I recoiled from his anger.

"Do murdered animals count as a 'murder case'?" Filter. I needed a better filter. Why didn't those internet stores carry mental filters to stop me from talking?

"YES! Since you got kidnapped and everything, YES!"

"I'm sorry. I shouldn't have blackmailed you into letting us come. You were right. It was dangerous, and I put not only my own life in danger, but Jen's also. I won't do it again."

For the second time tonight, I managed to make the person driving stare at me too long.

"Road! Please watch the road and not me!"

He swerved a little to correct for the car's drift, before tapping his finger on the wheel.

We sat like that for a minute.

"What are you thinking about?" I broke down and asked.

"My life choices," he rumbled.

I wasn't sure if that was 'yay, he loves me and was uprooting his whole life to move to Barrow Bay' or a 'how did my life choices lead me here' kind of statement and I was afraid to ask which one.

Silence.

"So, we're over the whole yelling bit?" I asked cautiously. This seemed too easy.

"You apologized."

Really? That was all it took? One little apology and he was over it? I looked at him. His jaw was clenched, and his knuckles were white where he gripped the steering wheel. Nope. I didn't think that we were done with this subject.

"I'm going back to the city. Tonight."

"Wait. What? Because I…?" *Snickerdoodles.* He was leaving me again.

"No. I have a case. I made a promise before I met you and I have to follow through. They already pulled me off this case and will be sending in another contact to work with the FBI. But it means I'll be out of touch for a while. Can we talk again after I get back?"

I was still processing the storm of emotions that he had brought with that speech.

He was leaving.

Then why did he kiss me? I mean, I didn't force him to. He made that choice. Several times. Then I acted a little stupid, and he just threw the towel in? I was getting dumped.

Wait, promise? He made a promise before he met me? That implied that he wouldn't have made it after he met me? He might still like me?

Talk. He wanted to talk. He sucked at talking. Was I going to risk this again?

"Lark? Can you hear me?"

I looked over at him, surprised to notice he had continued while I thought. "Yes."

"I can't get out of it. I wish I could tell you more because I know I'm—" He paused, his jaw clenching. "I know I don't let people in. And I want to let you in. But this case can't wait." He held his body rigid, but the glances he flickered over at me showed he was unsure.

This case sounded very important. I guessed that made sense if they were pulling him from a task force with the FBI. We should probably focus on that and not my emotions. Really.

"What does 'talk when we get back' mean?" One day I would listen to my own advice.

"That we need to have a serious talk when I get back." He hesitated before hitting the steering wheel and making me jump. "No. No more talk. I don't do well with talking. A date. We need a date. With food. And me picking you up. And kisses. A date. When I get back." He didn't look over at me, but I could see his eyes drifting over quickly before turning back to the road.

Huh. An official date. With food and everything. And I was pretty sure he was nervous about my answer.

"That was a very specific list."

"I had a lot of time to think about it on the drive after you were kidnapped."

Wow. Guilt and a date request. How could a girl say no?

"Yes. So long as there's food."

"And kissing."

I fake-sighed. "Like a dog with a bone."

"It's a good bone." He sighed when I snorted. "That didn't come out right."

"Nope. But it's a date anyway."

"And you would be willing to wait for me to come back? No dating other people anymore?"

"You're pushing it." But I was really okay with that, and the smile on my face told him I was teasing. "Okay.

No dating other people." I hesitated, trying to hold back the giddiness at his demands. "Until you get back."

He shot me a quick grin before looking back at the road. "I won't have a lot of access to cell phones for the next two weeks, but I promise to call you when I can." He smiled at me. "I promise a good morning message whenever I can, even though it might not be every day."

He remembered my list.

I nodded. I could accept that.

CHAPTER 16

The rest of the drive was shorter, because I fell asleep after a few minutes. I was contemplating all the meanings behind Brecken's words. How did he really feel? Was I reading too much into them? Next thing I knew, Brecken was waking me up from the door of the passenger's side.

"Do you know that you snore?" His amusement was a little heavy.

"I do not." I absolutely did. So did Hailey. It was a curse. Blake used to sleep with ear plugs. "I have no idea what you're talking about."

"Right." He didn't sound like he believed me. Smart man.

I looked past him to see that we were parked in front of Gran's house. "I thought we were going to the station?"

"You were asleep. We had a voice recording of everything that happened because you have gotten very good at calling John every time you get in trouble." That went a little bitter there at the end.

My calling John when I'm in life dangerous situations might have stung him a little. Oops. I used that moment to get out of the car, trying to avoid answering him. He followed, coming around the car for my explanation. Oh, goodie.

"You were busy, and John doesn't say anything until I do. He'll sit there for a while, just in case. I made him do it once to find out how long he would wait. Call him once in a bad situation and he teases you about it for the rest of your life."

"It's going to get worse now that you have done it twice."

I shrugged. "I'm okay with being a damsel in distress. Maybe he might get there before I rescue myself next time. He also tells me how to leverage the threat of lawsuit to get a hole in my barn roof fixed, so you know, he's useful."

"Still bitter about getting shot at?"

"Yes, and even more so that she shot at my horses."

"You still got the job done. We got there after you had already tied her up with bailing twine."

"Twice saved me. Stupid mare has more guts than I do."

He laughed. "I still have no idea what you're talking about. Sweetest mare ever."

"You just say that because she likes you," I mumbled, glaring at him. She was my horse. I fed her—well, I paid for her to be fed. I rode her and took care of her. I gave her treats and turned her out. She should like me more.

He laughed for a second before his gaze drifted over my shoulder. I heard the door open and close. Gran must have known he was leaving since she didn't say anything.

"I need to go," he whispered, his arm reaching out to wrap around my waist and pull me a little closer.

"Are you sure?" Oops. I wasn't supposed to say that. I was trying for mature and supportive, not needy and clingy.

He nodded. "I'm sure. But I want one more memory before I leave." He pulled me even tighter, pulling me flush against him as his head dropped to within inches of my face.

And stopped. Whyyy?!

"Are you going to kiss me?" I asked, trying to ignore how breathy my voice sounded.

"I'm debating how much ammunition to give your grandmother. Should I dip you and kiss so that she can get a picture, or will just a kiss get her to remind you every day I can't, that I'm coming back?"

"For the love of..." I grabbed his head and kissed him.

His arms tightened around me like he didn't want to let go.

Good. I didn't want him to.

He slowly released me, drifting back, and I let him go, chanting 'I will not be clingy' as he walked to his car. My chanting may have gotten louder as he got in the car and drove away.

"Wanting him to not go isn't clingy."

I jumped when Gran's voice came from beside me. I guess she had walked up as I watched him drive away.

"It's nice that you guys are official. It's about time you had a boyfriend again. I'll have to text Lindsey so that she can get a new article out."

"What?! No!" Boyfriend? ARTICLE? "No! Whatever you are thinking about doing, stop right now. Put your fingers up and step away from the phone."

Instead of listening to me, Gran took off towards the house. I waited for a second, taking in her flight. I was kind of proud. She was spry for seventy-three.

"We're not official!" I called out after her.

She stopped and turned to me. "So, you're single?"

Snickerdoodles. "I'm not, *not* single." Did that make sense? Not single meant taken, and we were not boyfriend and girlfriend, so yeah? It worked?

"Did you just say you're not, *not* single?" she demanded. She didn't wait for my confirmation, however. "That's the stupidest thing I have ever heard. Either you're single or you're not. This is some of that 'it's complicated' mess that I hear about on the TV and social media, isn't it?"

Well, I would say it's more of a divorced-single-mother-who-had-already-jumped-in-too-fast-and-gotten-burned thing, but that was just me. I wasn't ready to jump. I was ready to dip my toe in. Maybe swirl it around a little. Since he could kiss like a fiend, maybe sit down and put both legs in. But I wasn't ready to jump.

"We're dating. Just dating. No titles. No promises. Just dating."

That earned me a disappointed look. "Lark, honey, Benny can't wait forever. You need to get Brecken to commit to the job. Alice wants to go to the Bahamas next year."

Did she just... and she thought that I was going to chase after some man because Benny wanted to retire?

"I'm not dating anyone because we need a new town Chief!"

"But—"

"No!" I stomped past her, walking into the house in search of Hailey. After tonight I needed to make sure she was alive and happy.

"Lark, dear, you are being unreasonable—"

"NO!" On the other hand, maybe Hailey could help me hide Gran's body. She was seven. Body hiding could be a... life skill.

"But—"

"Hailey? Where are you, sweetie? I need help to ignore Grandma."

"She's in her room. Blake called me when you weren't home and didn't answer your phone. It's almost nine, Lark. She went to bed." Gran gave me a look that told me we were going to talk about this again.

"Good. I'm going to go sleep with her. Goodnight." I didn't want to recap tonight. Maybe if I ran away quick enough she would let it go.

"Don't think I've forgotten about this, Lark. Alice has plans to travel and Benny is getting too old to run around after criminals. Lock that man down."

"Still not happening!" I opened Hailey's door and shut it in Gran's face. My daughter was sleeping quietly in her bed and didn't wake up when I came in. I slipped closer. I almost died tonight. I almost deprived her of her mother. I needed to hold her.

"Mom?" She woke up enough to recognize it was me before snuggling up and falling back to sleep.

This was heaven, and I was going to stay here as long as she would let me.

***

The next morning, Hailey must have woken up and slipped out of bed early since the bed was empty. I knew that her warmth was missing next to me, but it wasn't enough to get my tired, overly drained body out of bed.

It took Gran knocking on the door to get my eyes to even crack open slightly.

"Lark! John's here. He needs to talk to you."

"No." I blinked a few times, trying to make the clock focus. I thought it said eight-thirty, but the eight was blurry. So was the three, for that matter. Really, I was guessing the first two numbers. The only one I was confident about was the zero.

"Lark. Did you get *kidnapped* last night?" Her voice was hard and angry.

Oh, fudge buckets.

"I'll be right out!"

"Now. And don't even bother saying you have to get dressed. You never got undressed."

I looked down. She was right. Thank God, I only wore sports bras, or that would have been uncomfortable. I slowly climbed out of bed and opened the door.

"Now before you even start—" I was going to go on the offensive, but she had the better hand.

"You got kidnapped?"

"A little, but—"

"There's no 'a little' when it comes to being kidnapped! And this right after the whole body thing! What are you trying to do to me? To your little girl? What would we have done if you died?"

Wow. She was on her guilt A-game. "I didn't plan for either of those things to happen. And Laura hunted me down. Not the other way around. I don't go out of my way to be in dangerous situations. I was with Brecken. Yes, it was a crime scene and yes, the guilty party decided to make a getaway in the only non-black-and-white car there, but I didn't do it on purpose!"

"I can actually confirm that. While she did force herself into being in the car," this earned me another disapproving glare, this time from both of them, "Lark and Jen did exactly what Brecken asked. It was just pure dumb bad luck," John said from behind Gran.

"Thank you, John." *I think.*

"So, I have a few questions and then we can get through what happened after you and Brecken left."

"Coffee." Because if they wanted me to think this early in the day, coffee was needed.

Gran doubled down on disapproving. *Shiitake mushrooms.* I hoped she hadn't found my secret stash and thrown it out. I needed something stronger than tea this morning. Every morning, really.

"I already have a cup made. It's sitting on the counter in the kitchen where you'll be doing your interview."

"I don't suppose we could have some privacy for the—" John started to ask before Gran interrupted.

"No."

John nodded and kept his mouth shut. Wise man, our John. We both followed her to the kitchen.

"You had to come here last night," John whispered the accusation when Gran had pulled a little further ahead and presumably couldn't hear us.

"Don't blame me. I fell asleep. Brecken made the decision," I whispered back.

He gave me a sad look. "Should we talk about what happened there?"

"At the vet hospital? Sure—"

"No, with Brecken."

Wait, what? "What do you mean? He had to go home." Didn't he? "Did the FBI agents go home, too?"

"They left this morning." He didn't meet my eyes.

"John, what are you saying?" I wouldn't say that I was getting a little anxious, but I was getting a little anxious. Did Brecken lie to me? Were all the kisses lies, too?

"Brecken turned down the job. Benny talked to him last night, and he said he couldn't take it right now. That he had commitments that came first."

Ahh. His sister. Their court case. The secret, very important case. I nodded. "He does." It was real. He wasn't fake. I could breathe again.

"Wait… you know what the commitments are?"

"His family. He won't leave them."

John's eyes unfocused, his hand rubbing his chin as he processed this information. "His family, huh?"

"He didn't tell you guys?" Oh, no. I'm a horrible not-not-girlfriend. He had told me a secret, and I had just blurted it out. "Please don't tell him that I told you."

"Your secret is safe with me. Or really, Brecken's secret."

We reached the kitchen, and I rushed to the mug of coffee sitting on the counter. One sip and I was in… hell. This was awful. Like, really bad. No wonder Gran hated coffee. Maybe she thought this was the only way to make it. Now I had a truly horrible decision to make. Drink it, because bad coffee was still better than tea, or throw it out and go without caffeine. I swallowed. But only because tea would be worse.

"Okay, John, what do you want to know?"

"What did Connor mean about the 'chip'?"

Random, but okay. "Most purebred horses are chipped with a microchip in their necks with their identification. These chips are needed for international showing and travel as well. Bon would have gotten one with his information on it when he was a colt, after DNA confirmation of his parenting. I don't know how they were intending to fake it for sure, but my guess was that Emily's mount didn't have one and so they were going to implant a new one into his neck with Bon's information, but they were trying to use a hacker to get into the system and it failed."

"Is it that easy?"

"No. It takes a hacker better than the one they found and some money to get into the system to change the numbers, but it's easier than trying to remove it and implant it in another horse. That might permanently damage the horse."

"Interesting." He jotted down some notes. "And you have known Emily a while?"

"Only through the show circuit. We were friendly at shows. Not someone I knew well."

"Would it surprise you to find out she was losing clients, and that Abby was her biggest, and almost only client, before she left?"

"No." Oops. That sounded mean… "Not really." Sigh. I could try for less mean once the coffee kicked in more.

"Why?"

"She's a decent rider, don't get me wrong, but her ego outranks her skills and she tends to be immature. All trainers go through that at some point. The point where we realize that we always have more to learn, and that our poop smells just as bad as the rest of the world's. She just took longer to hit that wall." Frankly, until moving here and opening my own business without my husband's reputation to bolster mine, I hadn't made that realization either. It was a sucky one.

"Why didn't she just tell Abby about the horse's death originally?"

"That was one of the questions I was hoping you would be able to answer. I'm guessing she needed the money too much and guessed at Abby's home issues. I don't think Abby is going to rush out and get another horse quickly, so Emily would have been down a hefty part of her paycheck. Have you asked her?"

"We did, and she told us the same thing you did. I just wanted to see if it was logical."

Great. I have become the go-to horse expert. Hopefully they didn't need me to psychoanalyze western riders. I was going to be useless. Horse people were not all the same.

Well, we're all crazy. We just express it in different ways.

"Did she tell you where to find Bon?" Or his body, I guess.

"Yes. Teams near her barn are working on that now. I'm handing it over to them since animal cruelty isn't my thing. Nor my jurisdiction." He shook his head at the thought.

"Is any policeman's specialty animal cruelty?" Wow. That was rude. "Sorry, John. That was uncalled for. You guys were all over Bon's death and I shouldn't have been criticizing you."

"We were all over it because of the potential insurance fraud. Not because of the horse's death. I get how that would make you bitter." He sighed. "The truth of the matter is, had the horse not been insured for so much money, we probably wouldn't have cared. And you're right to point out that it's wrong. That these animals who lose their lives due to human malice or criminal action should be higher on our priorities."

I nodded, one, because that was more than I expected and two, because I knew how hard it was to get a horse to be taken away for animal cruelty. Anyone who had been around private horse properties had seen it. The horses that were always skin and bones. No water. It amazed me that we could lose a well-fed, well-taken-care-of horse like the real Bon to colic, and yet some of these animals could live in hellish conditions for months. And no one cared.

Well, that was not completely accurate. We had yet to find a way to legislate what abuse constituted without making it punitive to own a horse. But we would keep trying.

"Why did Connor get involved? Other than he was dating Emily." *Slime ball.*

"I guess the real Bon didn't completely die of colic. Connor messed up when he gave him some medication and he had complications. Connor already had some malpractice issues from Washington and he was afraid that he would be run out of the business altogether if anyone found out another horse under his care died."

Yeah, that explained a lot.

"And Bon? The fake Bon? Did they confirm what he died of?"

"The police lab confirmed high levels of barbiturates and a sedative in his system. That's the chemical that is used most commonly to put down horses, right?"

"Yep." At least Connor had done it humanly. And that explained the wet spot on fake Bon's neck when we were loading him. Connor had given him the shot and then helped me put him in the trailer. Evil. "The Oleander?"

"They did confirm that there was some in his system, so like you originally said, he must have eaten a little and then stopped. It was enough to make him sick, but not deadly."

"Did they find out where it came from?"

"Turns out that Tony had decided to visit the ocean that day, and just happened to be in Barrow Bay the evening that the fake Bon got sick. And we found some in his car. Connor told us he just took advantage of the situation."

"Why?"

"Turns out that Tony found a loophole in the frozen accounts. If he could get the insurance payment, he would have enough money to run. Looks like he didn't look at the investigation's stipulation very well, though."

My head bobbed as I took all that in. Coincidence and an overabundance of murderous intent. Poor fake Bon. "What about the first rounds of testing? The ones that were incorrect?"

"From what we can tell, he never pulled blood to run the tests. He just faked the report and sent it in to the insurance company."

"And Jen? What's happening there?"

"I *can't* tell you that the FBI is done with their local investigation and will be leaving this morning. And I *can't* tell you that Tony's looking guilty as sin, but they need to put some last pieces together before they charge him. I also *can't* tell you that he'll be facing an animal cruelty charge since we found Oleander leaves in his car and caught him on some traffic cameras in the area the afternoon Bon got sick. The lawyers will figure out what they'll do about the attempted insurance fraud."

"So Nic's just leaving?"

John sat back in his chair, looking at me through narrow eyes. "I thought you and Jen didn't like him," he commented.

I debated my answer. If I admitted that I thought Jen liked him too much, I would be dropping her into a whirlwind of matchmaking she would not be prepared for. Then again, they sparked. Maybe it would be good to see if that spark would lead to a forest fire or a lifetime relationship.

"I liked giving him a bad time. Jen liked… well, let's just say that she claimed to hate everything a little too much for it to ring true. I'm the master of denying the truth. I can see it in others." I was either the best best-friend ever or the worst. Fingers crossed that it would turn out to be the first option.

John just laughed at me. "You're saying you think they might like each other?" he demanded.

"No! I would never admit that out loud. Never."

He laughed again. "Lark, for a girl who pretends that she likes to mind her own business, you sure like to stir things up."

"I know. I got the whole, 'if it weren't for you pesky kids' speech and everything." I smiled back. "Then again, someone has to do it."

My phone went off, alerting me to a text.

Brecken: *Good morning, beautiful.*

Thank you for reading Stir Up, book two of the Lark Davis Mysteries. The next installment will be coming August 2019. Click here to receive updates about upcoming releases.

WANT TO KNOW
MORE ABOUT JEN?

Here is a preview of Number's Up, a Barrow Bay
Mystery.

I had ruined my life.

Which was a problem, because I, Jennifer Ward,
MBA, CPA and business consultant, liked my life.

The minute I opened my door to a giant in an FBI
coat holding up a piece of paper, along with a black,
square-shaped object, I knew it. I blinked and both were
gone, but I assumed from the paper it was a badge.

An FBI agent plus a warrant? Yep. I had ruined my
life. Stupid morals.

"Jennifer Ward?" He waited for my nod before
continuing. "My name is Special Agent Nicholas Kelly.
I'm with the FBI. We have a warrant to search your
house and office." He scanned me before one eyebrow
lifted. Like Spock. Just like Spock from *Star Trek*.
Damn. I was not going to admit how sexy that was.
"Also, as much as I appreciate the view, it might help if
you put on more clothing."

This was a learning experience. Leggings and a
camisole with no bra didn't cut it for the FBI
investigative team. Any other time, I would have
appreciated him letting me change. Today? Today, I was
too mortified to think rationally, which was my excuse
for snapping back.

"I'm sorry I didn't dress to impress. What's the normal dress code for letting the FBI search my house and home office? An orange jumpsuit and a straitjacket?" *Oh, please don't let my lawyer hear that I said that. He might fire me as a client right then and there.*

He took another long look, running his eyes up and down me as he thought, his lips twitching slightly upwards. I had amused him.

I ignored the tingles his gaze caused. I was not going to find someone like him attractive. Nope. With a ready smirk, relaxed stance, and confidence seeping out of every pore, here stood a charmer, a lady's man, a rake. I had gone out with bad boys before and this man was all bad. He probably had plenty of girls at every stop. Ones he never thought of after he was gone. I didn't need another bad playboy. They were never as much fun as I always hoped. This giant version was not going to make me crack. I wanted a nice man. Responsible. Faithful. That was what I was looking for. Someone loyal and boring.

"Well, I don't think orange would be your color, but it's your choice." Then he stopped, his eyes stuck south of my face, a slight ring of red coming to his cheeks. "Yeah, I would definitely recommend changing."

I looked down and ran away. Tingles and no bra were a bad combo. Abandoning the door, since I couldn't stop them anyway, I made a beeline to my bedroom, because a bra was needed, and it was needed now. I made sure my bedroom door was closed before I took off my camisole, grabbing a bra and a more conservative blouse from my closet.

Why was everything I owned fashionable and form-fitting? I didn't want to be cute right now. I wanted to be... was there a word for unattractive without being actually unattractive? If not, there should be. Unisex? No, that wasn't right.

"I can't actually have you in the house without supervision. You might be destroying evidence in there," came the deep voice through the door.

"You open that door and I may have to kill you." He wouldn't open that door. Would he? I froze staring at the knob, praying that it didn't open before I got my shirt on.

Shit. If I had limited time to get dressed, freezing was the wrong call. I pulled the shirt over my head, sweeping my hair into a messy bun instead of brushing it into a neat ponytail and jumped to the door, swinging it open before he could.

He was on the other side grinning at me. "You know, threatening a federal agent is against the law."

"I'll take my chances," I muttered back. "What do you want?" Stupid question. I stood behind it anyways.

"We have a warrant to search your home and office for evidence of insider trading from one of your clients."

Today's federal agents were a gift from Tony Harris himself. I would have to thank him with a basket of snakes the next time I saw him. Non-poisonous ones, of course. I wasn't stupid enough to kill him. Just maimed a little. Tony Harris was a horrible man that my firm had been representing for years. Up until a few months ago, when we dropped him due to conflicts with his business account.

Those conflicts really had been me, not that I told Henry that. Finding out that Tony had been doing insider trading and that my partner had been covering it up had really broken my trust. As far as I knew, no one had found out who reported it in the first place.

No one knew I had betrayed them. No. I reported them. It wasn't betrayal. It was morally right. It just felt like betrayal.

I needed to clean something. Anything. There had to be something to clean.

"Fine." My lawyer had been very clear on this point. *Don't bother the federal agents. Let them look at anything they wanted to.* But that didn't mean I couldn't try to maintain some control. Maybe I could try to protect my other customers a little bit. "Tell me what files you want—"

"Not how this works, sweetheart. You sit over in the living room and I will be over to interview you."

Sweetheart?

Oh, no. Uh-uh, nay, nope, negative, vetoed.

I could feel my face turn hot, but I bit my lips together to keep anything stupid from coming out of my mouth. I was a professional. I could stay calm and respectful.

I would just let him know that I would not be condescended to like that. Not in my home. I didn't care if he was a six-foot-six giant of a man with the most beautiful hazel eyes that I had ever seen. His eyes started out blue on the outside, before a starburst of brown exploded in the center, spreading out like someone had spilled golden paint.

No. He was condescending. A bad boy. And he thought that I might be a criminal. He was not a dating prospect.

Also, I would not be relegated to the couch as his team of… of… *people* came in and… did their job. That rant went downhill quickly. It didn't matter. I was still angry. I wasn't going to let logic stop me. My life was going down in self-created flames.

"I will not be told to sit down like I'm a criminal." Again, maybe that wasn't the best argument. Since my business partner might have been a criminal, and all. "Fine. I will wait in the living room." No, that was too easy for him. I couldn't let it go like that. "After I make some tea."

"Some tea?" he asked, his head tilting to the side slightly. "What kind of tea?"

"Like you care." I stomped away, trying not to notice that he was following instead of meeting with the other FBI agents mingling around my house. I was attempting to not obsess over the fact that I didn't let them in.

Or that they were moving my stuff. I had to admit, though, they were moving it very carefully, searching through items before putting them back in place where they found them.

Which was weird, right? I mean, on TV shows, the police and federal agents would tear everything apart trying to find the missing information. The people in my house were polite. Yes, they were going through my stuff, but slowly. Methodically. Then returning it to near the same condition.

It was weird. Appreciated, but weird.

But still, I hadn't let them in. They just came in.

Court-approved entry. They were in charge. I was in hell.

I made it to the kitchen, where I pulled out my loose leaf tea brewer and started putting together a cup of my vanilla Ceylon tea. Hmm, I hadn't worked out today. Maybe I should go light on the sugar? I loved my curves, but currently I was a little too curvy, right around my waist.

"What kind of tea is that?" he asked as he stared at the brewer.

Now he was going to make fun of my tea. He was probably a coffee drinker. I looked him up and down. Black. I was willing to bet he drank coffee black, sugar and crème being too wussy for an agent like him.

"Does it matter?" Scratch the diet. I could already tell that this was not a diet day. Extra sugar. Maybe it would improve my mood. And my disposition.

"I guess it doesn't. I was just curious." He meandered through my kitchen, picking up things and then putting them down.

"I don't have any evidence in here," I snapped. I needed to calm down. Calm and professional. It was expected that they would look around my house. This was their job. This wasn't their fault, it was Henry's for helping to commit a crime.

And maybe a little mine, for betraying and turning in my mentor and business partner for that crime.

I turned to face the counter as my heart constricted in my chest.

"Probably not. I was just getting to know you a little more."

"And what have you figured out?"

"Workaholic, but I knew that from your work hours. Neat freak." He nodded around the room, pointing out that everything was in its place, every dish cleaned. "Single, and from the look of the book collection, chronically so."

I felt my face flush at his last statement. Yes, I was chronically single. My last boyfriend was a huge, cheating, man-whore mistake that I tried not to think about, and Barrow Bay wasn't the best place to try to attract a man. I looked at the dating self-help books he referenced. I knew how many there were. Six. Six times that I had decided to take my own happiness by the horns and find the love I wanted. I had failed. No, it was worse. I'd barely tried.

The real problem was that I worked too much. It was hard to compete with girls that actually remembered their accounts and responded back when it came to online dating. I would get lost in work and forget to respond. A lot. It was almost as bad as how often I forgot to buy groceries. I looked around. Which I hadn't done this week, either.

"Hmm, no protest?" He watched me closely, waiting for an outburst.

I wasn't going to give him the satisfaction.

"Contained." He took a step towards me, meeting my eyes with a slight smile. "Meticulous." Another step. "Detailed." Another. "Passionate." His voice trailed off as his last step took him next to me, his body inches away from mine. I lifted my chin so I could keep his gaze. "About your job. The perfect accountant." His voice had lowered to a whisper. I was slightly dazed by his proximity.

Why was he so close?

He leaned closer to speak into my ear, his breath sending shivers down my spine. "I don't trust perfection. It's always hiding something. What are you hiding? Are you as morally bankrupt as your partner? Does your pretty face hide a black heart?"

I was so focused on his body and his breath it took me a moment to understand what he said. He stayed next to me after he asked his question, holding me in his spell for a second longer than I should have given into. He smelled so good. Spices and musk. I couldn't stop myself from taking a deep breath before the moment broke.

"What?" Did he say I had a black heart?

Was he… did he just try to seduce me in my own kitchen? While his team looked through my house. For a confession? How. *Dare*. He.

I opened my mouth to lay into him.

Ding.

He lifted a finger to tell me to wait while he answered his phone.

Did he just…? And I actually stopped…? No.

"Nic." He grunted into the phone.

I watched as he nodded a few times, listening to the person on the other side of the phone.

"Right. I'll be there in a few." He hung up and turned to me. "I have to go, sweetheart, but I will be back."

"Don't call me sweetheart," I ground out between my teeth as he began walking away.

"Why? Are you not sweet?" He sent me a smirk over his shoulder.

"Because you will never find out." My teeth were clenched so tight that my jaw hurt, but I hadn't cracked completely. "Those of us with hidden *black hearts* are picky in who we let taste us."

Oh my god. That sounded better and way less dirty in my head. Way less dirty. Like epically less dirty. Shit.

His smirk spread over his face. He turned and walked back to me, crowding me once again to see if I would take a step back.

I didn't.

I should have, but I didn't.

"You, *sweetheart*, might be worth the taste. Also, you might want to clear out while we search. It's going to be a while." Then he spun and left.

He was everything I was taught Satan would be. Temptation wrapped in a package that would destroy me if I took the bait. So I wouldn't.

I hadn't backed down. But I didn't think I'd won that battle.

WANT MORE BARROW BAY?

Visit me at <u>AnnabelleHunter.wordpress.com</u> and sign up for my newsletter to get a free short story.

Made in the USA
Las Vegas, NV
08 August 2021

27808976R00152